THE EARL WHO ESCAPED
VICTORIAN ROMANTIC MYSTERY

ALL THAT GLITTERS

TAMMY ANDRESEN

Keep up with all the latest news, sales, freebies, and releases by joining my newsletter!

www.tammyandresen.com

Hugs!

PROLOGUE

LADY ELLA CARTWRIGHT stood dutifully at the bottom of the stairs next to her sister, Fern, her hands demurely folded. Outwardly, she was the picture of calm and serene compliance. But inwardly, she waged war, a tumult of emotions seething beneath her calm exterior.

"Hmmm," Lady Vivian Sanbridge murmured with a narrowed-eyed glare. Her stepmother was no fool and surely saw through Ella's charade.

They both knew the truth...Ella's compliance was a fraud and her stepmother only pretended to care about her stepdaughters. But neither could outwardly accuse the other. They had to pretend peace and harmony.

"Tell them, Mother..." her stepsister, Melisandre, huffed from behind her mother, her arms crossed and bottom lip stuck out. "Tell them that I know I left the ivory-handled brush on my dressing table and now it's gone."

"Hush," her stepmother soothed automatically, her gaze never leaving Ella's.

Ella posed her features into a sympathetic mask. "Are you certain, Melisandre? Perhaps it fell?"

1

"I checked everywhere." Melisandre pointed an accusing finger over her mother's shoulder, her brown eyes growing hard and angry.

"Your dressing room?" Ella asked in a false attempt to appear helpful. Melisandre's dressing room was, in fact, Ella's childhood bedroom. Ella had been moved to a tiny back bedroom in order to make way for Melisandre's mountain of dresses, shoes, and jewelry.

Melisandre huffed. "Of course I checked my dressing room." Her lip curled into a sneer. "We all know you took it, Ella. Why you insist on denying these things is beyond me. Why don't you just admit what you've done and take your punishment?"

She had no intention of saying any such thing. Nor did she plan to be punished. "Sister dear, why would you say such things about me?"

Fern looked at the ceiling, knowing full well that Ella had absolutely taken the brush. She and Fern each had their subtle ways to protest their stepmother's tyranny. Thieving happened to be Ella's. Fern's was far more direct.

Melisandre threw up her hands, her much larger arms and embellished sleeves looking like wings behind their stepmother. It wasn't that Melisandre was overly large. She was likely perfectly sized, but it was more that Ella and Fern weren't well fed. They were both small by comparison.

"I say those things about you because they are true. You're a horrible, no good, dastardly—"

"What's that?" Ella and Fern's father called from the top of the stairs, and all four women turned to meet his gaze, Melisandre falling silent.

Ella kept her perfected veneer solidly in place. She'd learned long ago that her father was not an ally in this quiet war being waged under his roof. At first, he appeared sympathetic enough, hugging her as she'd complained about their stepmother's cruelty, even as he told her to get along with their new family. That blending the two together would take time.

But he seemed to turn a blind eye to her and Fern's inferior clothing, their lack of food, their simple rooms, and the fact they had almost no lessons. After nearly a decade of living under her stepmother's rule, Ella had learned to fight back subtly and with plausible deniability, a lesson Melisandre had never learned. She didn't have to. Her mother smoothed away all of Melisandre's sins. "She's accused me of stealing her brush, Papa. As though I don't have my own."

"Of course you do," her father answered, coming down the stairs. "It was a present I gave you last year for your birthday."

"Exactly." She gave her father a bright smile. "Which makes it more precious than any jeweled piece."

"The brush wasn't jeweled," Melisandre pouted. "It was ivory."

"Oh, of course. I must have forgotten what it looked like," she lied, knowing full well that the brush was tucked under a loose floorboard beneath her bed.

Her stepmother's lip curled into what could only be described as a sneer even as she spoke for her father's benefit. "If Ella says she did not take it, then she did not."

Her stepmother, on the other hand, knew how to play her part well with her husband. She told him all the things he wished to hear, and then did exactly as she wanted with Ella's father seeming none the wiser. The woman absolutely thought that Ella had taken the brush, and she'd do her utmost to prove her theory and then punish Ella. But the countess would do so quietly...

Another swell of anger rose inside Ella. How did her father not notice that all the pin money went to Melisandre? Or that Melisandre received all the new dresses? All the lessons?

"Of course my sweet Ella didn't take your things, Melisandre. We're a family, after all." He smiled at his two daughters, Fern giving him a glare back. If Ella played the game, Fern froze everyone out with stoic silence and icy glares.

Her father didn't respond, however, and his eyes rounded and his shoulders hunched, wracking coughs seizing his lungs.

Ella truly winced then. There was no acting. Despite everything, she loved her father, and besides—what would life be like without him? Would her stepmother toss them out? Marry them off to some toads?

Ella stepped closer, wrapping her arm about her father's shoulders as he gasped for breath. "Relax," she whispered. "Try to breathe."

"My Ella," he said between coughs, his head coming to her shoulder. "My sweet Ella."

Melisandre snorted, a sound Ella pointedly ignored. When her father had recovered, he straightened, looking at his wife, the disagreement over the brush already forgotten. "When does Lord Pembroke arrive? I'm anxious to meet my heir."

"Soon. No later than a fortnight," she answered, placing a hand on his arm. They all knew the truth. Her father was dying. It was only a matter of time.

One might think that her stepmother's light touch on her father's arm meant that she cared, but Ella knew the truth. All her sneaking had earned her loads of valuable information over the years, but none better than what she'd gained two nights prior. Her stepmother had a plot. She was going to attempt to marry Melisandre to Lord Pembroke, soon to be the new Earl of Sanbridge. She'd already falsified at least one letter to Pembroke, using her father's seal and suggesting that Pembroke should marry Melisandre. Lady Sanbridge would do all in her power to maintain her control over the earldom. Lying to the heir was just the beginning.

Ella didn't recall ever meeting Lord Pembroke and, if she had, it must have been when she was very small, before her mother passed away. Which is why she didn't feel the least bit sorry for her own plans.

Ella gave her first real smile of the morning. She had a plot as well. And it was her best yet. She wasn't just going to steal a silly brush, or even a dress that she reworked into her own. No.

She was going to pull off the biggest heist of her life: she planned to steal Melisandre's groom. And it was going to be magnificent.

CHAPTER ONE

ELLA'S PLANS, however, were much delayed.

First, because the viscount never came, but her father's death did...

She'd held out some hope that her father might convince the new earl to marry either herself or Fern. That he'd finally acknowledge what a spoiled girl Melisandre was and that at the very end, he'd redeem himself and save them.

But no.

Her father had left her to fight her stepmother's schemes with no one in the world to look after them.

Two months had passed, summer had arrived, and the heir was nowhere to be seen. At least not here at Castleton. In that time, Ella had privately shed many tears for the loss of her father, the life she'd lost, and the future that looked so murky and grey.

If the new Earl of Sanbridge did not arrive, how would Ella escape Vivian's plans? Not that she knew exactly what the plans were, but she did know that whatever her stepmother did with her and Fern, it would certainly make their lives dreadful.

Anger filled her as she lay alone in her small bed. What right did Vivian have to take everything from them, even the love of their father?

And what could Ella do to get it all back?

Silently, she rose from her bed. Not bothering with her tattered dressing gown or even slippers, she opened her door and crept down the hall. She didn't need a candle.

Down the stairs and to the second floor, she moved into the bedroom next to Melisandre's. She knew this room well, as it had been hers once upon a time. Crossing to the wall that separated it from Melisandre's, she silently lifted a portrait from its hanging place to reveal a hole in the plaster.

Though a picture hung on the other side as well, she could still hear.

"He's finally coming," Melinsandre gasped with delight, her hands clapping together. "Are we ready for him?"

"Of course we are, dear. I wouldn't have summoned him if we weren't."

Interest made her lean closer, her breath holding in her lungs. Who were they ready for? The new earl?

"I can hardly wait. My shoes and dress should arrive any day now. Do you think we'll have the wedding here?"

"Melisandre," her mother's voice cut through the air, "you must be your most gracious self."

"Fine." Melisandre's voice had taken on a pouty tone. "Though we both know I hardly need to convince him. You've made certain I am the only choice."

Ella's eyes widened. What had they done?

"Still. Keep up the pretense. It's better if we don't need to back him into a corner."

Her breath caught as her thoughts swirled with possibilities. She'd have to find out, and then she'd need to decide how she was going to enact her plan. Because this was one time that Vivian was not going to win...

———

LORD ERIC HENDERSON, Viscount Pembroke, yawned, which in turn made his head throb, as his carriage rumbled along a country road toward Nowhere, England.

He jested. The place had a name, and he knew it too...it was to be his home, after all. But his head pounded from all the ale he'd drunk at the inn the night before and his thoughts were covered in a haze.

Scrubbing his face with his hands, he wished he had some snacks, and a large cup of water, and perhaps another ale.

He sniffed the air, noting that something smelled rather stale but as he pushed into a more upright position, he realized that the smell was wafting off his own clothes.

Though a viscount, Eric had never been much for propriety, and he stayed as far away from polite society as he could. He didn't fit with those people. Never had. He'd learned that in his school days and he was happier for avoiding them.

He scratched at his stubbly chin, smacking his lips to clear away the paste in his mouth.

The sun was casting a soft light in the sky, the sort that meant it was either sunup or sundown, but he had no idea which. Had he slept the day away or awoken after only a few hours of drunken sleep? He couldn't say.

"Driver," he called, thumping the head of his cane against the wall. "Where are we?"

"Essex," the driver called back.

"Where are we going again?"

"Essex," the man said again, having the decency not to laugh.

"Shit," he murmured, sitting up straighter in his seat. "How long until we arrive?"

"Minutes? An hour?" the man said.

"Will we pass through any villages?" He desperately needed a bath. Despite his devil-may-care attitude, not even he would arrive in this state as a guest. He knew he didn't deserve their hospitality, especially in his current state, but his hosts didn't need to be apprised of his unworthiness. At least not within the first minute of his arrival.

"Did already, my lord. Should I try to turn the carriage?"

Eric let out a soft groan as he flicked open the curtain. Turning the carriage took space and could be tricky depending on the road. But in the last rays of the sun, he noted a river up ahead. "No need, just pull over."

He'd not be able to shave, but he could freshen up at least, change his shirt.

With that in mind, he had the driver stop to the side of the rutted country lane and then he stepped from the carriage, making his way down the steep bank, his Hessians sliding in the dirt. It was nearly summer, but a stiff breeze still chilled his skin as he stripped off his coat, waistcoat, cravat, and shirt. His footman tossed him a cake of soap, and then, kneeling, he plunged his head and neck into the freezing water. It cleared a great deal of fog from his thoughts and as his head emerged, he began to scrub.

He briefly considered stripping off the rest of his clothes, but the road was open and, in the distance, a large estate rose into the twilight. He debated for a moment as he stared up at the stately mansion.

Was that to be his new home? He belonged there even less than he did in Pembroke, his ancestral seat. The thought of Pembroke made him grimace and he scrubbed harder.

He could hear the footman taking down his trunk from its spot on the back of the carriage, undoing the latches. "Reeves, I've changed my mind, I'll take a new set of breeches as well. These ones might walk away on me if I wear them any longer."

He may as well make a decent impression. He wasn't just coming here to meet the earl, who was a distant family member and whose earldom Eric would inherit, he was coming here to meet a bride.

He scowled at the idea. Him. Married. It suited him even less than sobriety, society events, or that giant estate with its rising spires. But he wasn't certain he had a choice. Well, he always had a choice. But this earldom had thousands of people who depended upon it, and his distant cousin, the former earl, had suggested just before his death that his stepdaughter would be most suited in aiding him in managing such holdings.

Considering he'd still be responsible for his viscountcy, and he'd been failing epically in those duties, and with the mountain of debt weighing down the title, marriage to the right woman would be a great help. He scrubbed at his face as he thought of the letter from his solicitor he'd received a few months back. He'd learned the hard way that one couldn't rely on hired help. What a fool he'd been.

Which is why marriage might be a boon. Provided the woman understand his parameters. This was no love match, and he was never going to be the doting husband. He'd keep his activities discreet and that was about the most he'd promise.

And she would help him to run their holdings with all the skill and intellect he lacked.

All straight in his mind, he kicked off his boots and waded into the water, still in his breeches. He'd give them a wash on his body and then he'd kick them off, scrubbing quickly before Reeves delivered him fresh clothing.

His stomach grumbled, likely complaining that after all that ale, he'd not had a bite to eat, but he ignored it, scrubbing at the material until, satisfied, he started to unbutton the falls.

"Oh my," a feminine voice called. He instantly stood up straight, one hand holding the breeches together as he scanned both riverbanks.

And that's when he saw a young woman lying in the grass. She was propped on one elbow, her golden hair shimmering in the dying sun. Her body sloped to a narrow waist before her hip flared, creating the most enticing feminine line. "I beg your pardon, madame. I did not—"

"It's quite all right, Lord Pembroke," she called back before rising from her spot and moving toward him. "Or should I call you Sanbridge?"

Her body swayed with such fluid grace that he was mesmerized for a moment, long enough that she'd nearly reached him before he realized that she held a pasty in each of her hands. "Pembroke will do for now. How do you know who I am?"

That's when his gaze rose to her face and every muscle in his body clenched. Even in the growing darkness, he could make out the clear

9

blue of her eyes, her adorable little upturned nose, her sweet, full mouth. She looked like an angel. "I make it my business to know most things that happen at Castleton. And your visit is much anticipated." Her words rang of something devilish despite her appearance and he found his brows rising as he assessed her from his position down in the water. He was still shirtless, not that he cared, but he watched as she took him in with her gaze.

Despite being a terrible drunkard, he still found time to box and ride. Physical activity was the only other outlet to the ceaseless turning of his thoughts, so he knew she'd noted all his muscles and he watched her gaze skim over them. "And who are you to make such things your business?"

She was a picture of contradictions. Her accent was fine but her dress simple and rather worn-looking. Her face had all the grace of a lady, but she was slender like a servant who worked hard and was given precise rations.

"No one of consequence," she answered with a wave her hand, the enticing pasty still resting in her palm. "At least not anymore."

"No one of consequence?" he asked, with a furrow of his brow. "That's no answer at all."

"Hungry?" she prompted, sitting once again in the grass as she gave him a smile. "I brought an extra."

He was famished and his stomach gave a decided gurgle at her offer and the sight of food. "Your name, madame?" He narrowed his gaze, determined to feel as though he had some purchase in this conversation.

"Lady Ella," she answered with a sigh, conceding to his demand.

"Lady Ella?" he asked, moving toward her, one hand still holding his falls together.

"Eldest daughter of the late Earl of Sanbridge."

"Oh," he said, working his way up the steep, wet ground toward her. "I see."

But he didn't really. Was his head still muddled? Because in the letter he'd received a fortnight ago, the earl had suggested that he wed his stepdaughter and here was his real daughter, looking more beautiful than any woman he'd ever met and yet her name had never even been mentioned. How odd.

And then there was her appearance. Nothing seemed to fit.

"Do you? Oh good. That will make everything easier." Then she held out the pie. "Come eat, my lord. You'll need your strength."

His brows rose as he reached up to take the pasty. Her delicate fingers brushed his as she gave him the loveliest smile. But despite her shining white teeth, or maybe because of the ominous words, the gesture of warmth didn't quite reach her eyes.

CHAPTER TWO

ELLA WATCHED him swallow down his meat-filled pasty in two quick bites and then she wordlessly held out the other.

His stare was wary, and she gave him a look of encouragement as she reached even closer. "Here. You're hungry."

She kept her voice gentle, her movements slow, not unlike what one might use on a stray dog they wished to tame.

With equal slowness, he reached for the pasty "You don't want it?"

"Dinner will be served shortly," she said in her most soothing voice. And tonight, because of their guest, she'd be able to eat a full meal.

The cook had been preparing for two days now, which also meant she'd been able to take several goodies as they cooled. A rarity. But she'd snitched these pasties anyway, part habit and part plan, because she'd hoped to catch the new earl before he arrived at the house. It would be so much easier to start on her plot if she could speak with him first.

Of course, it had been a distant hope, but here he was. Bathing in the river and living up to his reputation as a degenerate rake. At least that's what Vivian and Melisandre had said. But if his morals were loose, all the better for her.

Her gaze flicked over the width of his shoulders and down the muscular planes of his chest. His face was a bit pallid, like a man who drank excessively, but his body...

He reached for the second pasty, his large hand dwarfing hers, his skin several shades darker than her own. Her breath hitched at the juxtaposition. She'd always been small and a bit pale. In contrast, he looked large, strong, and...handsome.

His dark eyes glittered and his jaw tightened, their gazes holding. Something flickered inside her, warm and completely unwanted. This man was a means to an end, no more.

Another voice reasoned that if she managed to succeed, he'd also be her husband, but that was a consideration for another day. If years of plotting had taught her anything, a good criminal planned well but measured success one small step at a time.

"Thank you," he said as he took the pasty and stuffed the flakey pie in his mouth. Some of the color was returning to his cheeks with the food.

"You're welcome," she murmured with a dip of chin. "If you need anything else during your stay, please ask. I'd be happy to be of assistance."

He eyed her with a long stare, his head cocking to the side as he chewed. "Most gracious, Lady Ella."

But his gaze was weary as he dipped back under the water. Well, it took time to domesticate strays, she thought as she stood back up, shaking out her skirts. She had a few potential strategies in mind and as she shook, she considered which might be best.

Seductress, that was her first. The problem with this plan was that she had very little skill in the area.

Victim, that was the second. Which was the truth and so likely the most convincing. But it would require the mark to be sympathetic to her plight. It would also be more difficult to keep her real feelings masked. This was an arrangement in which emotions should be kept out.

A straight-up negotiation was her final option. She knew with absolute certainty that she'd make a better wife than Melisandre, who was spoiled at best and would likely spend what little was left of the earldom's fortune.

Some combination of the three, perhaps? Smoothing her hands over her hips, she watched the viscount's gaze follow her hands. Yes. Seduction was in order.

"I should return to the house before I'm missed," she said, giving a delicate clearing of her throat. "When we formally meet, I'd appreciate if you did not mention this little tête-à-tête to my family. They would not approve."

His arms crossed over his chest, which left his falls open, and the fabric drooped down his hips so that she could see the cut lines and corded muscle that gave way to hair... Her gaze snapped back up to his. Perhaps she was less prepared for seduction than she needed to be. "Then why did you come?" he asked, not sounding the least bit soft or swayed at all by her words or gestures of kindness.

She dipped back down, crouching so that they were closer, her words quieter. "You're to be my new lord, my lord." She batted her eyes, hoping that her face was set in sweet and innocent lines. "I was most curious."

He harrumphed. "I see." And then he relaxed a bit. "And I appreciate the food. It was a help."

She nodded, her breath hitching as she scooted just a bit closer. "And I wished to share with you..." Her tongue darted out to wet her dry lips. She didn't have to fake her nerves here because this was delicate business. If she said too much, he'd grow suspicious of her, too little and her words would lose their intended effect. "My stepmother..."

She paused, searching for the right thing to say.

But the earl spoke before she could finish. "Is she the reason your dress is practically rags?"

Well, didn't his observations make this easier. "I'm afraid to admit how right you are."

He frowned. "Is she also the reason you're so thin?"

He'd noticed, had he? She winced, knowing that even willowy

beauties weren't as thin as she was. "I manage to acquire the food I need."

His brows lifted. "The pasties you gave me?"

She blushed, half artifice and half real. "The cook has been in the position since my mother was alive and leaves food on the windowsill for me and my sister, Fern, whenever she can."

The truth was that Ella had grown crafty at taking enough for both of them.

His face darkened with clear irritation, and she noted that playing the victim would definitely be an asset. Which would not require much playing.

"Anything else I should know?" He gave his head a shake and she saw that his overlong dark-brown hair had the slightest curl to it. It looked soft and inviting, unlike everything else about him.

She sank her top teeth into her bottom lip, widening her eyes. This was going exceptionally well. If she failed, perhaps she should become an actress to support herself and Fern. "I would not want to color your opinions, my lord."

He dropped his chin and gave her a long stare. "Obviously."

"I'm glad you're here." She looked at him again, meaning every word when she said, "I'm hoping you bring real change with your arrival."

———

ELLA'S WORDS echoed in his head as Eric finished bathing, changed, and climbed back in his carriage to make the short journey to Castleton.

Him? The force of change? He was fairly certain that he did not ever fix things, he only wrecked them. Was that the change she wished for? He doubted it.

Several candles now burned within the estate, giving many of the windows a warm glow as he stepped from his carriage. The place was picturesque, but the image that Ella had begun to paint of it was anything but.

Of course, there was the possibility that she had not told him the truth. There was a calculating edge to her gaze that left him to wonder…

He'd find out, he supposed. There was no turning back, he was to become the earl, and this would be one of his many properties.

With that in mind, he straightened his fresh cravat and started up the stairs just as the door swung open. A stately butler greeted him with a line of women behind him.

An older but elegant woman in an elaborate silk gown was first. Next to her was a young woman with brown hair and matching eyes. Her gown was equally extravagant, the red silk catching the light.

And then there was Ella. Here in the candlelight, she appeared even more lovely, her blonde hair shimmering as her eyes winked with familiarity. The same dress she'd worn earlier skimmed down her body now.

Next to her was a woman who was nearly Ella's identical twin. This must be Fern. The similarity between them was startling, with one exception. Ella appeared friendly enough, but Fern's features were cast into a glare. There was no other word for it.

"Lord Sanbridge. A pleasure," the older woman said and gave a slight nod of acknowledgment as she offered her hand to him.

"Lady Sanbridge," he greeted, bowing over her fingers.

"May I introduce my daughter, Lady Melisandre." The mousy girl curtsied with a giggle, the sound instantly grating his nerves, her ringlets bobbing as she moved.

"My lord," came her breathy greeting, her lashes blinking up and down as she openly assessed him.

"And my stepdaughters, Lady Ella and Lady Fern."

Both dipped into matching curtsies, and he bowed to them as well. By their faces, Ella and Fern were about the same as age as Melisandre, but while the two sisters held themselves with grace and reserve, Melisandre acted years younger, her breathy laugh making him grimace.

"Dinner will be served shortly, my lord. Would you care to join us in the sitting room or is a repose in order after your journey?"

16

A repose? He'd had one already, complete with bath and food. "I'd be happy to join you."

The older woman's eyes flicked to her stepdaughters, her mouth twitching down the slightest bit as she assessed them. Most wouldn't notice, but Eric did. He wasn't much for books and numbers, in fact he was truly horrid at them, but he'd made up for it in life by reading people. "Ella and Fern, I know you had a busy day, you're more than welcome to—"

"Oh, that's all right," Ella smiled brightly. "We'll stay for Lord Sanbridge's benefit."

"Please, call me Pembroke for the time being. It's the address I am accustomed to and it keeps things simpler."

"Thank you, my lord." Lady Sanbridge's mouth twitched again, a tiny furrow appearing between her brows. "And how thoughtful, Ella."

The entire group moved into the sitting room, where the late earl's liquor was lined up on the buffet in the corner. For the briefest moment, he considered pouring himself a glass, but he had a feeling that he'd need all his faculties tonight.

As if she'd read his thoughts, Lady Sanbridge crossed the room toward the buffet. "May I offer you something, my lord?"

"Water, please," he answered, raking a hand through his hair. Melisandre sidled up next to him, giving another giggle.

"Water? Really? I'd heard you quite the imbiber of alcohol—"

"What my daughter means is that we know most lords enjoy a good drink at the end of a long day and we have some of the best vintages of whiskey and port in all of Essex."

He didn't doubt it. The house sparkled inside just as it did out, all the furnishings covered in lush new fabrics, the mahogany polished to a shine. And yet the financial statements had spoken of an estate teetering on the edge of financial disaster, at least according to his solicitor. He'd been unable to discern... The urge to have a drink nearly overwhelmed him but he pushed it back down. He needed what little wits he possessed.

"I am fine, but thank you. I'm sure I'll have a bit of wine with dinner."

The countess gave him a wide smile. "You'll like the vintage I've chosen for the meal. It will pair with the fish perfectly. And then for the roast—"

He smiled, giving a quick nod, but he cared far less about the wine tonight and far more about the company. Still, he allowed her to finish, giving a single dip of his chin when she was done with her lengthy wine report. "Thank you for that and for your warm welcome."

One manicured hand rose next to Lady Sanbridge's face, giving a small turn as though she highlighted her words. "Melisandre and I will see you settled here and help you learn the particulars of the earldom."

No one mentioned Ella or Fern, but he found himself looking over at them both where they sat side by side on the settee, Ella looking pained while Fern just looked angry.

He didn't ask why they'd not been included. A picture was emerging and while he'd questioned Ella's motives for seeking him out, he'd not been here more than a quarter hour when every word she'd said had been confirmed.

"Tell me about yourself, Lady Melisandre. What do you do for fun?"

Melisandre let out an airy giggle. "Besides pianoforte? And embroidery?"

His brows knit together. Were those the important skills for a countess? "Yes. Besides those."

"Shopping," she started before her mother dropped a hand on her shoulder.

"Shopping for the goods that enable her to be an excellent hostess. Which reminds me. We ought to consider having a ball to celebrate your arrival."

"A ball? So soon after the earl's—"

"We should make our way to dinner," Lady Sanbridge cut him off. Which made him even more perplexed. Hadn't the earl only died a fortnight ago? He'd received a letter from the man just last week.

18

But that mystery was quickly abandoned as they sat down to eat.

At a normal table, there would be several plates of each type of food prepared and placed down the length of the table so that no guest would have to reach over another to partake in any dish.

But time and again, fish, beef, even roasted vegetables were placed at their end of the table where he sat next to Melisandre and across from Lady Sanbridge. Hardly any food was placed in between Ella and Fern. Neither woman said a word, so neither did he as he lifted the large platter of sliced roasted beef and placed it between the two women.

For the first time since he'd arrived, Fern gave him a look other than irritation. Surprise lit her wide blue eyes.

But Ella smiled demurely, lifting the serving fork and taking a slice for herself.

Fern did the same as the countess cleared her throat. "My lord, I'm sure you know that it is impolite—"

He cut her a look, sitting straighter in his chair. He didn't need lessons in decorum. His mother had been one of the most gracious women in all of England. "Shall we have a conversation about manners, Countess?"

Her mouth pinched but she didn't say more as all three younger women stared at him. Melisandre's mouth visibly hung open while Ella and Fern darted gazes between him and the countess. "I'm sure you know a great deal on the subject. Both of your parents were model peers. Participants in society, well respected and liked."

He knew exactly what she didn't say. Eric did not live up to their memories, a fact he was intimately aware of. But that was not a weapon he'd give the countess. "I agree. I was most fortunate to grow up under their tutelage." He meant the words. Wonderful people, his parents. If only he'd been able to follow suit.

He took another bite of the beef, the roast falling apart in his mouth. Still, he might prefer a pasty while swimming. The company had been much better.

He looked down the table at Ella, who'd been silent, realizing what he'd seen as calculating might have been just hesitation on her part. Her stepmother was a force to be reckoned with, that was for certain.

He'd have to find out more. What was happening in this house, and was the earl's suggestion that Melisandre would be an aid a truth or another carefully crafted fiction? There seemed to be so many.

He could only hope he was intelligent enough to unravel it all.

CHAPTER THREE

ELLA BARELY KEPT from rolling her eyes as Melisandre let out a shrill cry, jumping from her chair.

They sat in the early afternoon sun, with Ella having been tasked with polishing the silver while Fern was supposed to be helping. Mostly her sister sat with her arms crossed.

But Melisandre had been embroidering until a knock sounded on the front door, echoing up the two-story entry.

"They're here!" Melisandre cried, lifting her skirts and racing out the door to the grand stair.

Their stepmother followed. "Melisandre," Vivian hissed, a rarity when speaking to her daughter. "Do not let the viscount see you like this."

"Stop worrying." Melisandre waved her hand before she disappeared from view, her mother just behind. Melisandre's voice still echoed through the house. "What's been delivered? Is it them?" She was clearly ignoring her mother, a behavior that only Melisandre was capable of getting away with.

"Them?" Fern asked Ella, breaking her afternoon silence. She generally only spoke when the two of them were alone. "What them?"

"The glass slippers," Ella supplied, dropping the fork she'd been polishing. "For her wedding."

Fern cocked a brow. "Do you think the viscount was what they expected?" But Fern didn't wait for an answer as she continued. "Did you see the way he plopped the plate in front of us last night at dinner?" Fern gave a rare chuckle. "He's not going to be as easy to manipulate as—" But then Fern drew up short.

"Our father was?" Ella shrugged. "We'll see." That was the truth. She had yet to decide about the man. Pembroke had strength, so she'd give him that. But did he have the intelligence and will to stand against her stepmother? Vivian was a lot of things, but addle-brained wasn't one of them. The woman was smart as a whip, and she used all that intelligence to manipulate Ella's father and undermine her step-daughters.

"You don't have faith that he'll not be cowed by her?" Fern asked, scowling once again.

"I don't know, but until I do, I'll continue on the way I always do."

Fern rarely gave her opinion on Ella's plots, but this time she gave her sister a deep frown as she shook her head. "Don't touch the slippers."

Ella wrinkled her nose in irritation that her sister had already guessed her plan. "Why not?"

"Because." Fern let out a long, tremulous breath. "That would not be just a petty retaliation, it would be a declaration of war. Pembroke is Vivian's great hope."

Didn't Fern understand? "That's exactly why I must. She cannot marry Melisandre to him. We'll be doomed."

Fern rubbed the spot at the bridge of her nose before she dropped her hand to stare at her sister. "I love you and I appreciate all you've done for me, but you're not seeing this one clearly. We will not be ruined. In fact, it would be quite the opposite. He'll be our guardian. If you just make a friend of him, you might find that he buys us dresses for a season and sees us settled in respectable matches."

Ella huffed. "Since when do you want a respectable match?" And since when did her sister tell her not to punish their stepmother?

"I don't. But I'd take it over this..." Fern waved at the silverware Ella was polishing.

"And let Vivian get away with it? Stealing our entire future?" Her voice was rising to dangerous levels.

"Ella, hush," Fern said, leaning closer and dropping her own voice. "I understand you're angry. I'm angry too."

That was obvious. Fern wore her anger like a suit of armor. "Everyone knows you're angry, Fern."

"And so perhaps I've let enough of the emotion out, instead of holding it in, to see the situation clearly," Fern said, reaching for her sister's knee.

Ella winced, knowing her sister was likely right. All the petty little blows she managed to land did little to vent the rage that had built inside her. Her stepmother and stepsister had stolen their entire life and their future too. It wasn't the dresses or even the balls. It was their father, it was the husbands they wouldn't have, the lessons they'd never gotten, the dowries that Ella suspected had disappeared.

"She deserves to suffer, Fern."

Fern gave her knee a squeeze. "This is not a rescue mission then, Ella, to save our futures. It's a revenge plot." Fern jerked her chin in affirmation of her point, then removed her hand. "Be honest about that with yourself, and then decide if you want to proceed. For my part, I say we take whatever safe harbor the viscount offers and use it to leave here and never look back."

Dissatisfaction rumbled through Ella. She didn't want to let Vivian win. "But—" Footsteps on the marble staircase stopped her words as Fern leaned close.

"And leave those slippers alone, Ella."

Her lips pursed. "Fern." Even she could hear the argument in the single word.

Fern's gaze narrowed. "I mean it. It will lead to nothing but trouble. And this is me talking."

But Ella didn't have a chance to respond before Lord Pembroke, as he insisted he be addressed, appeared in the doorway.

———

Eric surveyed both sisters, their heads bent together, their whispers sounding…aggressive. Were they having a quiet argument? About what? Did it have anything to do with the racket Melisandre was still making?

Whatever lay beneath the surface in this house, it was as murky as disturbed water in a pond.

"I want to see them. I want to see them now, Mummy," Melisandre demanded in the foyer, but the noise easily traveled through up to the vaulted ceilings and into the doorway he now occupied.

His jaw tightened. Melisandre sounded more and more like a spoiled child. He'd come here to meet the family that he'd become the head of but also to assess a bride.

His shoulders grew heavy as he thought of all that he'd gotten wrong since becoming the viscount. His choice of wife could not be one of them.

Ella and Fern noticed him, their whispers ceasing, and both women rose from their seats, Ella giving him a bright smile as Fern glared.

"Do come in, my lord," Ella said with a curtsy.

Fern rolled her eyes as she sat back down without any ceremony. He walked toward them. "What are you ladies doing?"

"Polishing the silver," Fern answered, which took him by surprise. He'd yet to hear her speak since his arrival. Not at dinner and not at breakfast.

Even Ella looked startled as she turned to her sister with wide eyes.

But Fern held out a towel to him. "Would you care to join us? It's got to be done before dinner."

His brows lifted. "Why are the two of you completing the task?"

Ella put a smile on her face once again. "It's one of many tasks we complete. I'm sure you'll see why when you review the ledgers."

His brows lifted and Fern scowled at Ella. The rough outline of their argument was beginning to take shape. Did Fern not want Ella to give him any details about the house?

But he didn't have a chance to ask more because Melisandre sailed into the room, a wooden box in hand. "They've finally arrived," she said in a rush of air, crossing to the settee and plopping down upon it, her wine-red silk gown billowing out around her. It was in such stark contrast to what Ella and Fern wore, simple dresses meant for work, that he did a doubletake. Ella gave him a knowing smile as Melisandre continued talking. "It was ages ago that the measurements were taken to create the casts to have them made."

"What are they?" He didn't move toward Melisandre, sure she'd give him all the explanation required and then some.

"Slippers," she gushed, lifting the lid. "Glass."

He blinked, trying to think if he'd ever seen such a thing. He had to confess, he hadn't spent much time with society, despite living in London. He preferred gaming hells and back-alley watering holes. Men didn't talk of philosophy or politics there, they just drank and yelled. "I didn't know there was such a thing."

"They're not made often," Melisandre said as though it was the most obvious thing in the world. "They're special." Her pleased smile clearly said that she had them because she was also special. "And they'll be for a very special occasion."

Right. Suddenly he understood. Had they already begun buying items for the proposed marriage? Before he'd even arrived, they'd assumed that he would surely marry Melisandre?

He opened his mouth to disagree in some way, or just slow down whatever was happening. This choice of wife would take care and time on his part, and he'd take it more seriously than he had most things in his adult life.

He'd been drinking away his sorrow and wearing a façade of nonchalance, but now he was ready to be the man befitting the title, best he could, anyhow. And somehow, he had to marry a woman who filled in his...er...gaps.

But he'd be shocked if Melisandre was the woman to help him complete those goals. Spoiled and mean, was she casually cruel like

25

her mother? He needed a woman with some understanding and intelligence.

Lady Sanbridge entered, giving him a demure smile as she nodded her head. "How lovely you've joined us."

He responded in kind, but his eyes were drawn to the twinkling glass as Melisandre lifted one of the slippers from the box. It sparkled in the afternoon sun, looked beautiful and delicate and incredibly uncomfortable.

"Impressive," he said, his gaze narrowing as he wondered what kind of craftmanship went into such an item and what the cost might be.

Lady Sanbridge turned to her daughter. "They are spectacular. Not every woman could manage such an item with grace."

"How were they made?" he asked. They did not make Melisandre any more interesting, but the pieces themselves were quite stunning.

"I had to sit for hours to have my foot cast so that they'd fit perfectly," Melisadre stated, one hand covering her heart, as though it had been a trial. "But it will be worth it now."

"Melisandre, why don't you take those upstairs to your dressing room? We wouldn't want anything to happen to them."

"But I've not tried them on!" Melisandre cried, ignoring her mother's suggestion. "Bring in a footman to help me."

His teeth ground together at the whiny tone the woman took with her demands. A footman appeared, along with a maid, and one of Melisandre's slippers was removed while the glass slipper was put on her foot.

Or, at least attempted.

Everyone gasped as the slipper refused to slide on her foot. Ella rose from her chair, coming to stand next to him.

That's when he realized he had never been close enough to catch her scent before, but she smelled of summer wildflowers in the sun.

He drew in her intoxicating perfume even as Melisandre let out a cry. "What's happening?"

Lady Sanbridge bustled over to her daughter. "I'm sure it's nothing."

"Take my stocking off," Melisandre demanded. "Take it off now."

"Oh dear," Ella whispered. "This is not going to end well."

He leaned closer, drawing in a deep breath of air. He couldn't care less about Melisandre or her building tantrum. That seemed the only word for it when she let out another cry, shoving at the shoulder of the footman.

"Here we go," Fern murmured, coming to the other side of her sister. "Everyone be prepared to duck."

"Duck?" he asked, but then a pillow came sailing through the air and everyone dipped so that it flew past them and hit the wall.

"I cannot believe after all that, they don't even fit!" Melisandre had turned an alarming shade of red, and she yanked the slipper from the hand of the footman to hurtle it toward the wall on the same path as the pillow.

It sailed directly at Ella. Automatically, his hand shot out, plucking the glass shoe from the air before it could hit her.

"Melisandre," Lady Sanbridge bit out, her voice hard and sharp, so that not even Melisandre could ignore her. "Upstairs at once."

Melisandre stood with a loud huff, her skirts rustling as she stormed toward the door. "It's not fair," she cried, stamping her now single bare foot. "It should fit."

Lady Sanbridge followed her daughter silently from the room, making eye contact with no one as she disappeared.

Looking down at his hand, Eric had to admire the tiny shoe. He had no idea what an item like this might cost, but he'd imagine it was as rare and special as many jewels.

"Let's have a look then," Fern said, sitting back down. "It might be our only chance."

"Look?" he asked.

"At the slipper," Ella answered, sitting too, while the servants filed out. "Melisandre would never normally allow it."

"Ah," he answered, knowing full well that Melisandre got the lion's share of all the resources while these two received very little. For his part, he liked them both more for it. "How much do you think it cost?"

"Who could say?" Ella answered, then tilted her chin to the side. "Perhaps you will find out later."

"When I look at the books, as per your suggestion?"

She gave him a beaming smile. "That's right. Now, Fern, you first."

He handed the shoe to the tiny blonde, who only wrinkled her nose. "Can you imagine wearing this? It would hurt terribly."

"Are you going to try it on?" Ella asked with a small laugh. "Be a princess for a minute?"

"Goodness, no," Fern answered. "My feet are far too wide. They'd be bloody in an instant." Fern gave her head a subtle shake, her gaze holding Ella's meaningfully, silently communicating something to her sister.

Ella ignored whatever Fern was trying to say as she took the slipper from her, sliding her own shoe off and slowly pulling the glass onto her foot.

It fit like a glove, her toes sliding effortlessly into the footbed.

"It's like it was made for you," Fern said with a frown. "Though it wasn't," Fern stressed, leaning forward to inspect the treacherous glass.

"I know that," Ella answered, but still, Eric noted the warning from Fern, and he had to wonder. What was that about?

CHAPTER FOUR

ELLA LOOKED DOWN at the sparkling glass, the surface dancing in the light. Her chest was so tight, it was difficult to breathe.

It wasn't that she coveted the glass exactly. She didn't wish to wear these shoes, not ever. It was what they represented. Being loved, for starters.

Ella hated Vivian with a passion that boiled in her blood. But she could give her stepmother credit in one regard: she loved her daughter and she used most of her energy to fight for Melisandre. Not that Melisandre needed that kind of dedication at this point. In fact, it would be far better for her stepsister to be coddled less and become more independent. But these shoes were a living representation that Melisandre was cared for.

More so, the slippers reminded her of all the other resources that had been given to Melisandre. Money, social advantage, plans for the future...

They all belonged to Melisandre and each of those facets sparkled exactly like this shoe.

But the shoe had not fit her stepsister...

That honor had belonged to Ella. In her mind, that meant that perhaps every aspect of Vivian's plans for Melisandre might just belong to Ella as well.

At least if she was crafty enough to take them...

"Take it off," Fern hissed, tapping Ella's shoulder with several hard pokes.

Ella obliged, slipping the glass slipper from her foot. Not that wearing the piece mattered, Fern's request to take it off was too late. Ella's plans had been cast just as this glass had been made. Forged in fire and crystal clear.

What Fern didn't understand was that really, Ella would accomplish both their plans. She'd steal back what rightfully belonged to her and her sister and she'd win over Lord Pembroke so that Fern could have any future she wished.

Silently, she handed the shoe back to Pembroke. As he took the delicate glass, his fingers brushed hers. They were long and strong and yet elegant, his rougher skin masculine in the sort of way that made her shiver at his touch.

She withdrew her hand, dropping it in her lap and clasping the other as he crossed the room and placed the shoe back in the box.

"Is it always so interesting here?" he asked, his tone light, as though he were making a joke.

"Interesting..." Ella repeated glancing up from her hands to catch his eye. "I can say that it is rarely dull."

Fern harrumphed, likely angry with Ella but she wasn't worried about that. Her sister was her ally, whatever happened. They loved each other but they needed one another too, and that dependency glued them together.

"It's like a fox hunt," Fern muttered. "But ask yourself, who is the fox and who is the hunter?"

Ella knew that was another warning, one she fully intended to ignore because she was the hunter here and she'd caught the scent.

"I think the best person to put our family into perspective for you would have been our father," she said to Pembroke, ignoring Fern. "It's a pity you didn't meet him."

He closed the lid of the case and looked at her, his gaze searching. "I agree. I wish I'd been able to come before he passed."

"Me too," Ella said, wanting to ask him why he'd not come sooner. She knew her father had written to him months ago. "I know he wished to meet you too."

"I enjoyed his letters." Pembroke cleared his throat, surely uncomfortable. "And I'm sorry for you both. Losing a parent is never easy." Of course, he'd lost his father too. That's how he'd become the viscount.

"Did he write many to you? Our father."

Pembroke frowned. "Just the one, of course." He patted his pocket. "To say he was sick and that I should come."

Fern scowled as she picked up a spoon and began vigorously polishing. "I'm sure you had a great many affairs to settle before you did."

Pembroke, however, looked completely confused. "A few."

Ella shook her head. Hadn't Fern advised her to make friends? Was her sister really going to call him out on taking months to come? "It doesn't matter how long it took. We're glad you're here now."

"How long it took? A week is a reasonable amount of time for—"

"A week?" Ella was on her feet. "You can't mean that."

"What do you mean?"

"Our father died three months ago," Fern stated matter-of-factly.

The shocked look on Pembroke's face told her several points. He wasn't lying and he'd come as soon as he'd received the letter. "Did this letter also suggest you wed Melisandre?"

"How did you know?" he asked, his hand covering his pocket.

Ella shook her head. "I wonder if he even wrote it," she mumbled as much to herself as to Fern or Pembroke. "I doubt he'd have gone so far as to suggest you wed Melisandre. That smells of Vivian."

"Ella," Fern hissed. "Be careful making accusations you can't prove."

"Why?" Pembroke asked, looking between the two women.

"No one openly goes against her in this house without serious punishment," Ella added. "Except for Melisandre."

"Exactly," Fern said, stopping her work to give Ella another long, meaningful look. And then Fern raised her chin and looked back at Pembroke.

"And if I do? Question her motives or her actions?" he asked, managing to stand even straighter as he looked down at them.

"Prepare for Vivian's counterattack," Ella answered. "It will be brutal, so you'd better have a plan."

"What will the counterattack be?"

Ella didn't know. Not yet. But she had her ways of finding out.

———

THE LONGER HE STAYED HERE, the more certain he was that this house was rotten...

Perhaps he'd fit right in. His parents had been good people. Kind, generous, loving. But not even their good natures could make up for the fact that he'd not been born right.

Sure, he was strong, and he read people with relative ease. Fern, despite her quiet nature, was upfront and honest.

Vivian was a viper, Melisandre a spoiled brat, and Ella...

There was something well-hidden beneath her beautiful façade. What did it hold?

Or was that just his attraction clouding his normal perception?

Even now, she smiled at him, her face so innocent, but he was certain she hid something...

Or perhaps she really just wanted him to understand how awful her life was. She'd asked him to review the books. He winced at the idea. Despite being a lord and the son of wonderful parents, he was defective. Unable to calculate numbers and hardly able to read, he couldn't even manage the most basic reports from solicitors and property managers. Which was how he'd ended up with a thief among his ranks.

The man was being tracked down. One of his primary accountants, he'd stolen vast sums, all while Eric drank his way into a nightly stupor.

Shame filled him as Ella watched him closely.

He looked away, not wanting her to know the truth.

"My apologies," Lady Sanbridge called from the door. His head snapped up as he looked at the elegantly cold woman before him. Had she deceived him? Sent him a fake letter months after a man's death? He thought of how she'd interrupted him last night when he'd tried to mention the letter.

"Melisandre didn't mean to cause such a scene, my lord. She's been under a great deal of strain and with you here…"

Fern stopped polishing, casting her gaze to her stepmother, and Ella turned as well, her face a complete mask of indifference. "Overtaxed?" Ella volunteered. "Your visit is most exciting, my lord."

Lady Sanbridge's eyes turned to slits as she looked at her stepdaughter. "Yes."

Eric stepped between the women, his own plan forming. "It's unfortunate. I'd hoped to ask her for a tour of the property."

Ella cleared her throat from behind him. "Since Melisandre is indisposed for the afternoon, perhaps Fern and I could—"

"A tour is an excellent idea," Lady Sanbridge answered. "But I'll give it myself. Thank you."

Ella gave a single, almost regal nod, as Lady Sanbridge turned to him, smiling serenely. "Shall we?"

"Let's," he answered, following in the lady's wake. But he gave a quick glance back at Ella and Fern, cocking one eyebrow as he noted that Fern had leaned in once again and was furiously whispering to her sister.

But truly, he'd hoped to gain time alone with the countess. He had some questions. First, however, he allowed her to get comfortable. Remaining a step behind her, she began a monologue. "The marble here was imported from Italy. I chose it myself," she was saying, her hands clasped in front of her.

One didn't have to be good at math to know what something like that must have cost. "It's beautiful."

"Thank you." They continued, past the music room with the latest model pianoforte, to the portrait room where the ceiling had been painted in an elaborate fresco, and further into the house where one extravagance after another was brought to his attention.

"I have considered this house my personal canvas and I must confess, it's one of my greatest accomplishments," Lady Sanbridge said. "Besides Melisandre. She's developing into a rare beauty."

He didn't argue. "How long have you been lady here?"

"A decade," she answered. "The earl needed a wife to help him raise his two girls and I very much wished for a father for my daughter. It seemed an ideal match."

"Ideal," he murmured, knowing that the earl's daughters had suffered from the union. Not even his questions about Ella could disguise her obvious mistreatment.

They'd reached the sleeping quarters, several doors open to reveal large rooms, when Ella came down the hall toward them.

Between her hands was the box with the slippers.

"What are you doing?" Lady Sanbridge hissed, her voice sharp enough to cut glass.

"Delivering these to Melisandre," Ella said easily, using one finger to point to a closed door on the right. "I know she's upset now, but she'll want them. I'm sure of it."

Lady Sanbridge seemed to relax, but her smile was acid as she replied. "Very well. Put them in her dressing room."

With a nod, Ella opened the door, giving him a glimpse into the room that held rows and rows of dresses and boxes of every shape and size.

Ella returned moments later without the box, a large smile on her face. "How is the tour?"

"Good," he answered as Ella stopped in front of them.

"Excellent," she replied before she turned to her stepmother. "Shall I take his lordship about the grounds?"

Lady Sanbridge's lip curled, just the smallest bit. "That won't be necessary."

"Very well," Ella answered with an airy wave of her hand. "I'll be in the sitting room finishing the silverware."

"Do that," Lady Sanbridge said, watching Ella walk away. But they didn't move. And when Ella had disappeared, she turned to look at him. "That girl is trouble. I love my stepdaughters dearly, I do…"

He lifted an eyebrow. He doubted that very much.

She leaned closer, saying in a lower voice, "But stay away from Ella."

Lady Sanbridge didn't elaborate, and he didn't ask. Ella was right about one thing. His best chance at discovering the answers to his questions were in the books he couldn't read or by speaking to the man who had died. Which only left the books. "Can you show me to the earl's study?"

Lady Sanbridge's mouth pursed.

"The study? My husband's—"

"Mine," he returned, his patience wearing thin. He'd told them to call him Pembroke because he'd assumed that man had only died days ago, but it had actually been months, and now he was done with Lady Sanbridge's manipulations.

He knew he'd not accomplish much by trying to read the columns, but Ella's words were still ringing in his head. "And I thought to look at the books."

"The books?" Lady Sanbridge's mouth pinched and her face paled several shades. "What would you need to see those for?"

He cleared his throat. "The financial health of the earldom is of the utmost importance."

"Then take my assurance that the earldom thrives. The lands produce well, and the people work hard."

"I appreciate your words of comfort, my lady, but I'd like to see for myself."

She notched her chin, her gaze hard. "My word should suffice, and this house is still my home."

He paused. They'd gone from assurances to possessiveness. "You are right, my lady. But rest assured, I only wish to be the best earl I can be."

"Still. I can tell you all you need to know."

His hands fisted at his sides, frustration making his jaw as hard as granite. "I can find it myself if you won't take me there."

Lady Sanbridge gave him a long, slow appraisal before she finally relented, her hand sweeping toward the hall in invitation. "No need. Right this way."

CHAPTER FIVE

Eric sat staring at the books as though the numbers made sense. Pushing Lady Sanbridge to escort him to the study had been revealing, but the columns told him almost nothing. They blurred in front of his eyes as he shoved the heels of his hands into his sockets.

He wished they'd made sense.

If he could only decipher books, not only would his own lands be in good health, but he would understand what problems he was inheriting here.

But who could he ask?

He had friends in the city. The Duke of Westgate would surely help him. Or perhaps his friend Jacob. But both of them had busy lives and he'd never shared his problems with either of them. He was too embarrassed.

The one man he'd told, the man responsible for keeping his books, had used that information to rob him blind.

He'd taken more than forty thousand pounds in the last seven years. Until recently, it had never been enough that operations couldn't continue, only enough so that when Eric had gone to make repairs on the estate, he'd been assured by the bank that he'd have to make them on credit. There was not enough money.

He stood, crossing to the liquor table in the corner, and poured himself a healthy glass of amber liquid, swallowing it down in a single gulp. At eight and twenty, he thought he'd developed systems, hired people to make up for his deficits without ever revealing the truth. He'd been the viscount for nearly a decade.

And his secrets had been safe.

When he'd learned of the theft, Eric had allowed his solicitor to believe it had been neglect, rakish behavior, rather than admitting Eric himself was intellectually incompetent.

How could more lands and people fall under his care when he'd so completely failed the ones he already held?

"Going that well?"

Ella.

He refilled his glass and turned to look at her. Despite the faded blue gown, her fresh skin and clear blue eyes made her the picture of beauty as she stood in the doorway. "I can tell you one thing—your stepmother did not want me in here."

"No, she wouldn't." Ella entered and then softly closed the door behind her. "Which is why I shall give us a bit of privacy."

His brows lifted even as she made her way past him to go around the desk, waving him to follow. He did, genuinely curious what she might show him, while he took another swallow.

She looked down at the open ledger, her finger skimming along the columns. A minute passed and then two, silence stretching out between them. What did she see? Did she understand any better than he did? "Look here."

His gut clenched as he took another sip. "What am I looking at?"

She nodded as though it made sense to ask her to explain. "It's difficult to make heads or tails of when you have no reference points, I know, but here are all the house modifications."

Even he could see the large deductions, though he had no idea if they properly corresponded to the overall accounting. He came up right behind her, leaning over her shoulder so that her scent filled his nostrils. "Before my father grew ill, he tempered her spending, but

THE EARL WHO ESCAPED

lately..." And then she pointed to another. "Clothing and personal items."

"How much?" he asked, not able to add them all in his head.

"Thousands of pounds."

He looked at her dress, knowing very well who that money was being spent on. "What else?"

"Here." She pointed again. "Significant sums are being moved from other places into this one column."

"What account is that?"

"I don't know," Ella whispered. "But I intend to find out."

He raised his brows. This was the skill set he lacked. A woman who could see the information on the page, understand it, and correct for it, that was incredible. But beyond that, he liked this Ella. Smart, intelligent, and so lovely. If only he didn't sense some veneer that was meant to hide her intentions. "And how will you do that?"

She looked back over her shoulder, so that their faces were close. Close enough that he could see the flecks of green in her blue eyes, close enough that he could count the smattering of freckles over her nose.

Close enough that if he leaned down just a bit, he could press his mouth to hers. How would she taste?

Eric was no fool. Women found him attractive. Handsome, charming in his own way, he'd always had his choice of ladies.

And the way that Ella's eyes widened and then dilated, he knew in that moment that she would welcome his advances.

The numbers on the page might have been a blur but he straightened away, completely clear that it was best to keep intimacy out of this particular situation.

Not only were Ella's intentions and the details of her stepmother still murky, but Ella was a mystery he'd yet to unravel. Was she all that she seemed or were his instincts correct? She hid something under all those sweet smiles.

Ella might be intelligent enough to the be bride he needed, and she was certainly beautiful enough. There was an attraction between them. But the woman he'd wed also needed to be a moral compass for his land. He'd trust her with great swaths of his wealth, and he had to know she'd not abuse that power. He had a weakness and so he'd have to trust the woman he married to compensate for him.

He pretended to be carefree. It had always been the way that he kept everyone from realizing how inept he was. But his wife would know. She'd have to and he had to be able to trust that she would not do what his accountant had done.

With all that in mind, he eased back. "How will you find out what that column means?"

Ella winced. "My stepmother's voice carries, Melisandre's more so."

Did she eavesdrop? Despite the fact that he'd just been waxing about morality, if he were Ella, he'd do some careful digging as well. There was acting justly, which he appreciated, and then there was just plain shrewd. He didn't mind the latter as long as it kept within reason. "You'll listen in, will you?"

She shrugged. "Desperate times."

He liked her honesty in this moment. This felt real in a way so many of their interactions did not.

He gave a quick nod. "I understand—just be careful to not get caught."

That made her lips curl into a devilish smile, her angelic features looking even more beautiful like this. "I always do."

He thought back to the whispers between her and Fern. "Does your sister object to this kind of behavior?"

"Listening? No." Ella shook her head, returning to the books, her finger sliding down column after column as her lips moved wordlessly.

"If not listening, then what?" Because it was obvious that Fern did not approve of something. But Ella didn't answer as she bent closer, studying the book in front of her.

"What is it?"

She grimaced. "We seem to be operating on credit."

His chest grew impossibly tight. That's what he'd been afraid of. "I'll have to get my solicitor here to look at these."

"That would be a great help, my lord," Ella said. "Someone has to stop her."

The words were said with a tremble, the fear so clear that Eric lifted a hand to settle on her slender shoulder. "I'm here to keep you safe. Remember that."

She looked back at him then, a vulnerability he'd not seen shining in her eyes. "Fern and I have been so alone."

———

THE EASY PART of interacting with Lord Pembroke was that most of what she said and did wasn't actually pretense.

It was more about allowing him to see her true feelings in order to push him in the direction she wished for him to go.

But as he slid his hand down her arm and pulled her close, Ella had the sudden fear that she'd erred.

He had just offered to do what her father should have done...keep her safe. Would Pembroke fulfill his promise? She knew he'd try. Her father had tried, hadn't he? He'd just been no match for Vivian. But if he could have done more, he would have, wouldn't he?

Was Pembroke going to do any better? Or would he get caught in Vivian's web as well? And if he didn't? If Pembroke did all that he'd promised, would she deserve the help of a good man, the way she was attempting to marry him for her own plot?

All at once, she felt like Vivian. Hadn't that sort of manipulation been what her stepmother always did with her father?

Keeping Fern safe, that was one thing. But using this man for revenge...

He hooked his arm around her and suddenly she found herself pressed against his chest with her head tucked under his chin.

She'd seen those muscles that rippled down his body, but to feel them was another matter entirely. Breathless excitement sizzled through her, and she didn't know if such feeling was beneficial or not to her plan. She did know that she couldn't control the racing of her pulse.

41

"I see what's happening here," he said, a hand settling on her neck, the other wrapped about her back. "The way you and Fern are being hurt, and I'm going to stop it."

She prayed he did not see her own actions clearly. "Thank you," she whispered into his chest, her hand tentatively touching his narrow waist. Was this how it felt to be comforted and protected?

Her eyes fluttered closed as she breathed him in. The scent of leather and fresh air filled her nose. Had he been outdoors? His cheek brushed across the top of her head, and she tipped back to look at him, the strong line of his jaw, the prominent planes of his cheekbones. She caught the faint scent of whiskey on his breath. How would he taste?

It was a question she had never asked herself before about any man, and the shock of even wanting to know made her pulse roar in her ears.

She trembled and in response he flattened his hand on the small of her back, settling their stomachs even closer.

Her breath hitched, coming out in small bursts as her mouth went completely dry. "My lord."

"Eric," he said, the quiet rumble of his chest moving through her. "My Christian name is Eric."

Eric. Ella. Ella and Eric. The two names danced around her head, fitting together as well as their bodies did in this moment. "I…" Any words she'd meant to say had disappeared, replaced with a haze of pleasure. "I'm glad you're here. Fern and I…" She lost them again as she stared at his mouth.

The pad of his thumb brushed over her cheek. "I am the earl here, Ella, and you are under my protection."

She'd been under her father's protection too. That hadn't stopped any of what had happened. She wanted to believe her father still loved her, had deep down wanted what was best for her, even if he'd been unable to stand against Vivian.

But somehow, thinking of her father broke the spell that had been cast about her. Much as she'd like to throw herself at this man's feet and hope for protection, she knew that he might fail.

Which was why she had to rely on herself. "I appreciate that," she answered, giving him a smile that she didn't feel. "And I'll do what I can to help you as well."

"A partnership." He gave a quick nod. "I like it." And then he took a step back, cool air touching all the places that had been so warm against him.

She shivered as her gaze dropped to the book sitting on the desk. Her hand slid over the open page as she tried to make herself focus on this essential task. "I so rarely get to see what she hides," she murmured, clearing her head so that she might memorize as much as possible.

"I am sure we can arrange another viewing," Eric said, still close enough that she could lift her hand and touch his chest. She fought the urge. She'd not get mushy now and she'd not overplay her hand.

She shifted, her stomach tightening, thinking again of how she was playing a game. Wanting him for the purpose of thwarting Vivian and Melisandre. But that wasn't all true. Not anymore.

Still. Perhaps it would be better to tell him the whole truth...about how her father had never managed to stand up for them. How she planned to marry him just to turn the tables, but that...

That idea was also dangerous. What if he wasn't strong enough to face Vivian? What if he didn't approve of her plan? She could not afford to be vulnerable now. Everyone else had more power than her, her only advantage was cunning, and she'd give that up the moment she told him.

"I'd like that very much," she answered as she sat at the desk, determined to focus on the rows of neat columns. She'd stick with her plan, and she'd steal the groom. Not because she liked him, but because Melisandre did not get to have him.

CHAPTER SIX

Ella repeated these words over and over as she searched several more ledgers, attempting to determine where money was being diverted. The perfect scrawl was that of her stepmother's, smaller and finer than her father's handwriting, so Ella knew it was Vivian who'd been moving the funds.

But where was it going and for what purpose?

She drew in a tremulous breath as she searched another book, finding no hint of the sums she'd seen in the first book.

Eric sat across from her, drinking another glass of whiskey, having had too many of them to count.

He'd been silent as she worked, not interrupting in any way, but as she lifted her head to tell him of her frustration, his eyes drifted closed, and his head slumped forward. Was he drunk?

She grimaced. A good indicator that she should continue to rely on herself. The sun had set, and she had another job to complete before she went to bed this night.

Leaving Eric where he was, she slipped out of the study, making certain no one was watching as she crept down the hall. She'd return to her old room to see what she might hear. If she had to guess, her stepmother had spent the afternoon consoling Melisandre, who was likely still pouting.

A small blessing for Ella.

Making her way to the dressing room, she slipped in and first stopped to stare at the wooden box with the slippers. It sat atop a chest, exactly where she'd left it, the shoes still safely tucked inside.

Vivian had seen her carrying the box. She couldn't take them until Melisandre had noted the shoes here in her dressing room. Otherwise, it was too obvious. They'd still know she was the thief, of course, but she had to have reasonable deniability.

She briefly considered Fern's words and then Eric's. Both wanted her to depend on him, and allow him to rescue her. She shook her head as she looked away from the box, and then removed the painting from the wall once again.

For several seconds she heard nothing and then, when she'd nearly decided to leave, Melisandre spoke. "My dress is supposed to arrive tomorrow."

"Let's be quieter when it's delivered, shall we? Men like to think they have a choice, even when they don't."

"Just force him already. He's not going to choose me otherwise."

"He might," Vivian bit back, sounding annoyed.

"It's pointless," Melisandre pouted. "He doesn't like me. I can feel it."

"You haven't tried."

"He's already got his nose in the books. He's going to know some part of our plan."

Ella's breath caught. Would they say what they'd done with the money or where they'd moved it?

"I have to admit, you were right on that account."

"It doesn't matter," Melisandre said. "He'll marry me either way."

"He will," Vivian agreed. "He's exactly like your stepfather. A good man, but not the most intelligent."

"The easiest kind," Melisandre laughed.

Ella shifted in disappointment. She'd hoped to learn more about that money. Or some specific part of their plans. But also, she heard their vague references to manipulation and that feeling rose again, like she was one of them for also feigning interest in Eric.

Vivian paused. "I wooed your stepfather. I still think you ought to try the same. He'll be easier to do your bidding later."

"He's too young for that and not interested enough in me," Melisandre answered, her voice growing hard. "It's Ella who is catching his fancy, which is why the stick will be more motivating than the carrot."

Ella's stomach dropped. They'd noticed that he was interested in her? That possibility made her plan stronger, but clearly, they had their own and hours of eavesdropping had not revealed the particulars.

What did they plan and would her own be enough to best them? She stayed for another hour but learned nothing else of value.

Silently replacing the painting, she returned to the study to find Eric still asleep in the chair, his body slumped to the side.

She wasn't certain why she'd returned. Her conscience was smarting perhaps. Was she still using him if she'd developed real feelings? And what if she did marry him? Did she tell him she'd been angling for his hand as a point of revenge?

She touched his shoulder, but he didn't move, didn't stir at all, and so she circled the desk. She'd searched every ledger, but perhaps another was hidden?

Why not gain answers that might allow her to expose her stepmother without attempting to steal Eric?

Bending down, she felt the floor under the desk and then lifted the candle, looking along the shelves of books.

"Still searching?" Came Eric's slightly slurred voice.

"You're awake," she answered instead, turning toward him. "You should make your way to bed. You'd be more comfortable there."

He rose, stretching. "I can sleep anywhere," he answered, his lithe body on full display as his arms lifted over his head. "Habit, I guess."

She held the candle up higher. "Habit?"

He shrugged. "Drinking is a bit of a pastime for me."

She winced, wishing Vivian had been wrong on this account. She'd called Eric a rake and he was proving it true. But a habit like the one he described would make him far less able to go against Vivian. "And this works for you?"

"Not really," he said, his hands coming back down to scrub his face. "I've got to do better."

"Don't we all," she answered. He swayed on his feet, and she set the candle down, slipping to his side and grabbed him about the middle.

His arm came about her, crushing her to his side so that she wasn't quite certain who was holding up who. "You're very beautiful."

"Thank you," she said with a smile. This might be an excellent time to get some information from him. And utilize seduction. Guilt and excitement warred inside her. "You're very handsome as well."

"Thank you." He gave her a funny grin, one side of his mouth tipping up. It was charming and sweet, and she found herself laughing softly. "Though you needn't say so."

"It isn't polite to return a compliment?" She let her fingers drift up his chest, the feel of his muscles causing her own to tighten.

"Well." He looked up at the ceiling and swayed again. "I've had plenty of compliments over the years, while you…"

"I see. A man of the ladies."

"I wouldn't say that." He pulled her closer. "I mean, I do have a reputation, but much of it's been exaggerated to cover the truth."

"The truth?" Her breath caught. What would he reveal?

"I'm not very smart."

Her brows lifted as she looked back up at him. Was it her imagination or was he drifting closer? Was her plan working? "Eric, you can't think that. I know you're intelligent. You've sussed out the situation here, for example."

"People." He let go of her with one of his arms, swinging it around wildly so they both skittered to the side. "Those I'm all right with."

"What are you not all right with?"

He let out a heavy sigh. "It doesn't matter. What matters is I'm going to do better."

They swayed again and she tightened her grip about him, worried they were going to fall.

"How do you think you will improve yourself?" she asked, trying another angle.

He looked down at her, his gaze hooded as silence stretched between them. "Well..." And then he lifted his hand to cup the side of her face. "I'm going to start by marrying the right woman."

———

ERIC HEARD ELLA'S STUTTER, her slender arms about him.

Had he upset her with his words? What had they been again?

"So you are planning on marrying, then?"

Oh yes, that's right. "Yes. To the right woman."

"And which woman is that?"

Her voice had an edge, the one he didn't like. "Don't know yet," he said, noting that to his right was a very comfortable looking settee. He'd think better sitting and so he shuffled toward it, Ella still in his arms. "But she'll be intelligent in all the ways I'm not."

"And which ways are those?"

Reaching the settee, he turned so that he sat down, but he didn't let Ella go and so she tumbled down with him, landing on top of him. Her body pressed to his in all sorts of interesting places and he found his hand skating up her spine as she lifted her head to look at him. "Eric."

The breathy sound of her voice pulled at his stomach, making him harden.

"Despite what I said about other women, I'm not the sort to take advantage," he said, knowing that he was hardly making sense. But it was just that his body was responding in ways that his head said it shouldn't.

"Then why am I stretched out on top of you?"

"You're very beautiful."

"We've covered that," she said but a little smile pulled at her lips and her hand trailed over his shoulders, settling on his chest. "I'm more concerned about who you plan to choose as a bride."

But he wasn't thinking about far-off plans like marriage. He was focused on the immediate situation. He found a beautiful woman on top of him on a settee in a private room and...

He lifted his head, moving closer. "A bride..." What he planned to say next was anyone's guess. He had a far more interesting task he'd like to complete with his lips.

Rising up a touch more, he brushed his mouth across hers, his brow furrowing when she did nothing. She neither moved away nor pushed forward. Her lips didn't close or open, she was completely still.

He skimmed his hands over her neck, holding her jaw in both his palms as he tried again. Giving her the mouth the lightest brush, she remained still once again, but this time she let out a rush of air.

Satisfaction rumbled through him as he brushed his lips over hers a third time and this time, she kissed him back. Light, tentative, but a kiss nonetheless.

He gave her another, increasing the pressure the slightest bit, and then again, until she began to meet him touch for touch, her hands, which had been resting on his chest, twisting into his shirt.

Her mouth was so soft, her smell all around him, her skin velvet under his hands. He wanted more.

And so, slanting her lips open, he brushed his tongue along the seam of hers. She gasped, and suddenly, she was gone, her body off his in an instant, leaving his hands in midair.

"Ella."

"I..." she said, her trembling hands pressing over her hips and down her skirts. "I should go."

"Stay," he said, not sure what he hoped for. Distantly, he knew she was an inexperienced lady, and his ward at that. But he liked her in his arms. She fit against him so nicely and she was beginning to feel...right.

Then again, how would he know? Getting things right wasn't his strength.

"Good night, Eric. I'll see you tomorrow." And then she spun and disappeared again. He thought about going after her, but his body was heavy and his lids fell closed.

Tomorrow, he'd decide what part Ella played in his future.

CHAPTER SEVEN

ELLA PRESSED her back against her bedroom door, eyes squeezed shut. That kiss had been just so...she searched for the right word.

Wonderful? The word didn't even begin to describe what she'd felt. Magical.

That was the one. She brushed her fingers over her lips, her hand still trembling. She'd nearly lost herself in that kiss.

A deep part of her knew that Eric was an honorable man. She could have allowed him to compromise her right there in the study. She would have enjoyed it, even. But somehow...she just couldn't. She had too much to lose.

It was too dastardly, and her feelings were so complicated. She liked him, she might more than like him. Which in and of itself was an oddity. She never let anyone in, not ever. Fern was the only person she loved, because every new person in her life was a risk.

But Eric crashed down her defenses. She nearly smiled. She supposed he might be good at breaking down walls, he was very well-muscled. But there was something so decent about him. She wanted to believe he'd save her if she let him.

Which frightened her more than Vivian.

She wanted to trust him.

But trusting anyone else had never gone well.

She pushed off the door and changed into her faded night rail, unpinning her hair and loosely plaiting the long blonde locks, then slipping into her bed. It took an excessively long time to fall asleep, which was how she happened to sleep late.

Usually, she had her breakfast in the kitchen, long before anyone woke. It was her most dependable meal of the day.

But now, the kitchen would be busy, and she'd not be able to take any leftover food. She'd have to join her stepmother and stepsister in the dining room and hope that Vivian found no fault with her.

Dressing quickly, she made her way downstairs, hopeful that plates of food might have already been brought in, but her family had yet to arrive.

She was disappointed to hear Vivian and Melisandre's voices, drifting out to her. "I've a busy day today," Melisandre was saying.

"How so?" Vivian asked, sounding unusually sweet.

"A delivery and another fitting for those glass slippers." Ella's eyes widened. Once the glassmaker had come and gone, Ella would be free to take the slippers. Unless the man took them with him?

But her stomach turned. The idea of stealing them, of continuing with her revenge plan, made her shift uncomfortably. Was Fern right? Should she trust in Eric instead?

"You'll manage it all, I'm sure," Vivian replied with a trilling laugh. "You've so much grace in this regard, don't you think, my lord?"

"Hmmm," came Eric's deep baritone.

Ella covered her mouth to keep from gasping. She wasn't certain she was ready to see him. Not after last night.

But the alternative was not to eat. With a deep breath of fortification, she stepped into the room with a bright smile. "Good morning."

Everyone turned to look at her, shock on each of their faces.

Vivian and Melisandre were likely surprised as she never joined them for breakfast.

And as for Eric, was he thinking of last night, the way she was?

His jaw hardened, but he said little as she came in and filled a plate. With him here, she'd get to eat, at least. That was something.

But her stomach danced with such butterflies that she could hardly swallow a bite as she sat down at the table.

"As I was saying," Melisandre continued, "I'll have to sit for the glassmaker again. It's a trial, but perfection takes time and effort." She gave Eric her most charming grin. Was this her attempt at wooing him?

Ella looked at the ceiling.

"He's redoing them for you?" Eric asked, and he took a long swallow of tea. "How generous of him."

"Well," Melisandre grimaced, "he claims the shoes are to the original specifications but that a new, larger pair is our only option."

Eric set down his cup. "And you've pin money for a pair of glass slippers?"

Melisandre spluttered as Vivian held out a hand. "These will be for the ball, my lord."

"Which ball?"

Ella's eyebrows arched. They'd been for the wedding that Vivian had planned for a groom that they'd never even met. It was too ridiculous to say out loud or, perhaps, plans had changed.

"The one we're hosting, of course. As a welcome to you," Melisandre answered, sounding slightly annoyed, as though this information should be obvious.

"When was this decided?" Eric's voice bit out.

"Forgive me," Vivian said, touching a hand lightly to her chest. "I planned the event as soon as I received your letter, informing me of your visit. Did I not tell you?"

"When did you receive my letter?"

Vivian gave him a small smile. "A fortnight ago."

"And how long has your husband been gone?" Eric leaned forward, his eyes glittering dangerously. Ella's eyes widened in surprise. Was he trapping Vivian into admitting that she lied? Or at least withheld information from him for months about her father's death? How interesting.

Vivian's face contorted into a mask of despair. "Three months and five days," Vivian said and gave a delicate shudder. "We'd begun to lose hope that you'd come. Our relief was so great…"

Ella's mouth snapped shut. She should have known Vivian would lie her way out of the trap. Her father had asked Vivian to write to Eric months ago, but Eric had only received the correspondence days ago.

"Then why did I only receive your missive earlier this month?"

"Who could say?" Vivian waved her hand airily. "And had I known you would not wish for a ball, I would never have planned one, but…" She gave him a sympathetic glance. "It's too late now, the invitations have all gone out."

She watched Eric's hand close into a tight fist. He'd begun to understand what a slippery foe Vivian could be. His eyes met Ella's down the length of the table and she winced in sympathy.

He took a bit of his eggs before he looked at Vivian. "I want a full report of the guest list and the costs of this party. We're going to cut expenses wherever possible and that includes glass slippers. Cancel the appointment."

Melisandre rose, a cry of outrage falling from her lips, and Vivian frowned. "My lord, that is hardly necessary."

"Countess Sandridge, I'd like to see you in my study at the conclusion of breakfast. We need to talk."

Ella said nothing, but she most certainly was going to attempt to listen in to that conversation. She'd been waiting for years for someone to say those words.

———

ERIC KNEW that the hangover was not helping his mood, but Melisandre's insistence that being fitted for shoes somehow made her a worthy countess was more than he could tolerate today.

And he could not prove that Vivian had sent him the letter about the death of her husband months after the actual event, but he had his suspicions. She'd needed time between her husband falling ill and his arrival to move money, and once she'd completed the task, she'd sent him the letter.

But how to prove it? He knew he wasn't going to find the evidence no matter how hard he looked.

He rose from the breakfast table, his eyes locking with Ella's as he bowed to the ladies. His brow furrowed at the question in her eyes. Did she think he made a mistake with Vivian? But then a hazy memory from last night made him straighten. Ella on top of him, his lips teasing hers.

Christ. Shock rocked through him first, but desire quickly followed as he remembered the feel of her softness against the hard planes of his torso. Her hesitance, the feel of her hands balled into the fabric of his shirt. The taste of her mouth and the feel of her sigh.

He spun on his heel, knowing that he needed to collect himself. He'd speak with Ella later. Right now, he had to rid them both of her stepmother.

With that, he charged toward his office and penned a simple note to his solicitor, requesting the man's immediate presence at Castleton.

He summoned a footman just in time for Lady Sanbridge to arrive in his study. She entered the room, her eyes darting around as she approached the desk. "It looks exactly the same as it always has."

"I expect it does." Was she hoping for sympathy? She'd not find it from him.

She stopped at his tone, her head cocking to the side. "What is it you think I've done, my lord?"

His jaw hardened. "Besides dressing your stepdaughters in rags while your daughter has a wardrobe larger than the queen's?"

She pulled a handkerchief from her pocket and clutched it in her hand. "You're right. I can confess to preferring my own child."

He grimaced. "Is that why you don't feed them?"

"Did Ella tell you that? I told you she'd stir trouble. This was her attempt to do exactly that."

He scowled. "I've been at dinner. Your lies won't work on me."

She dabbed at her eyes, as though wiping away tears. "Lies, my lord? I'm so hurt."

"I've been through the books. You can drop the act."

"Act?" She dabbed faster.

"I've seen that column that is not accounted for anywhere else." He stood straighter, his chest puffing out. It wasn't in his nature to intimidate women, but he'd not allow her to believe she could manipulate him, either.

Her hand fell, her face turning to granite in an instant. "I don't know what you think you found—"

"You know what I found."

"Then you know that you'll have to marry Melisandre."

His brows rose, alarm rang in his ears. What had she done with the money and why did she feel comfortable admitting as much to him? "Tell me, why's that?"

"My husband saw fit to move much of the expendable money into her dowry. Without her hand, you'll never run this earldom."

Had Ella said how in debt they were? Not that it mattered. He knew two things, and the first was that he'd never marry Melisandre. Not only was she not fit in any regard for the position of countess, or his wife, but he found her personally repellent.

The second thing he'd realized in this moment was that his experiences with his own land and title had taught him something. He'd survive the debt. His solicitor could tell him how long it would take him to climb out of it, but he was strong enough to weather a storm such as this. Vivian's threat of financial ruin would not break him.

That made him smile and he saw Vivian falter. Good.

Not only did he enjoy besting her in this moment, but he also found a bit more value in himself. And that was a nice feeling.

"You do realize that I'm Melisandre's guardian and that makes me the owner of any of her assets. I don't need to marry her to collect the money."

"Won't you? Wouldn't you prefer to have all you needed for the viscountcy and the earldom?" She gave him an acid-filled smile.

"I'm made of sterner stuff than that. I'll marry whom I choose."

"And who is that?" Her eyes narrowed into slits.

This woman was a viper, and it would bring him a great deal of pleasure to strike back. "You know very well who I am going to choose."

Vivian's eyes turned to fire a moment before she spun on her heel and left.

But she'd only been out the door for a moment when he heard Vivian hiss. "You."

He made his way to the doorway in three quick strides, just as Vivian swept down the hall, to find Ella standing just outside the door.

"Hello," she said with a small wave.

"Listening again?" But the sight of her made him smile and he found himself holding his hand out to her. She slipped her fingers into his, small and so fragile. A wave of tenderness rose inside him.

"Maybe," she whispered as he pulled her closer, folding her into his arms.

"I think we need to talk about yesterday."

She shook her head against his chest. "We will."

"We kissed," he murmured into her hair.

"I know," she said into his shirt. "But let's worry about Vivian first and then we can talk after."

Her words made a great deal of sense. Pulling back, he reached for her hand again and guided her into the study, closing the door behind them. Once they were alone, he tugged her into his embrace again and leaned down close to her ear and whispered. "She's moved all that money to Melisandre's dowry."

Ella's fingers tightened around his. "But that makes no sense. You control any dowry and the distribution of it."

"That's what I said."

"And how did she respond?"

He trailed his fingers down her spine. "She didn't. She just stormed off."

Ella shook her head. "Vivian is a master manipulator and placing the money in a dowry is so basic. There is no way she didn't think of that."

Well, so much for his inflated self-worth. "So I didn't best her?"

Ella leaned back to smile up at him. "Sorry. I doubt it. But I lov— I appreciate that you tried."

"Do you ever try...to best her?"

Ella shrugged, looking away. "Not successfully."

He paused for a moment before he bent down and grazed his lips over her forehead. "Our combined efforts, then?"

"Oh, yes," she answered with an eager nod. "I'd like the very much."

"The question is how—how do we prove anything?"

Ella stared at him for the beat of several seconds. Then she gave him that devilish smile. "I have an idea."

CHAPTER EIGHT

ELLA TIPPED HER CHIN BACK, looking at Eric as a thought clicked in her brain like a lock turning a key.

The letter.

Vivian had sent it months after her father had passed. And the letter had referenced a match between Eric and Melisandre. Her father would have never written such things.

And Ella knew her stepmother's handwriting. She'd seen her neat and tidy scrawl half her life. She even had samples in the ledgers to prove to Eric that her stepmother had penned the letter.

Which would be a wonderful opportunity to change course. She didn't need to manipulate him into a match to best her stepmother. Well, she'd like for him to propose, but not because she'd schemed her way into the arrangement. Instead, she'd just prove her stepmother a forger.

It would be the first cornerstone in proving wrongdoing on her stepmother's part. If she could find one small act, a thread to pull from the fabric of Vivian's plots, perhaps the thing would unravel.

"The letter from my father," her words rushed out. "Do you have it?"

"Of course. Why?"

"He died three months ago. Long before you received the missive. What are the odds he wrote it?"

Eric frowned. "That doesn't prove theft."

"But..." She held up her finger. "It does defame her character and her absolute innocence is the heart of her defense, always. Beloved wife and mother. If you can prove she's forging correspondence and delaying the arrival of the heir, then you can create a solid argument that she used that time to steal the missing funds."

He gave a quick nod. "I'll be right back."

Without another word, he left the room, the ticking of the clock the only sound that filled the space.

Tick.

Tick.

Tick.

Tick.

Was she finally going to get the proof that her stepmother was not what she pretended to be?

Tick.

Tick.

Tick.

Could she return herself and her sister to their rightful place in the earldom, to a place of safety and comfort?

Her hands grew clammy as she pressed them together, her breakfast churning in her stomach. This was the moment she'd been waiting for. She'd best Vivian, she could give up on this plot with Eric and perhaps let things just develop naturally between them.

Not able to stand still another moment, she began to pace, her feet falling in time with the clock.

She knew the note had to be a forgery.

Her father would not have...

The door swung open and Eric appeared, quickly closing it behind him. She rushed to him, her heart hammering in her chest as he handed her the neatly folded letter.

She opened the paper as she crossed to the desk, her hands trembling as she prepared to set the letter upon its surface and pore over every word.

But she stopped halfway to the desk, a cry falling from her lips.

"What is it?"

"It's..." She swallowed down a lump, tears springing to her eyes. "It's..."

"What?"

Pain lanced through her as she struggled to breathe. "It's from my father." She could hardly get the words out as her eyes blurred, only phrases popping out at her.

"Your father?"

"He wrote it. I'd know his writing anywhere. His word choice." Her voice came out scratchy as she tried to read. He recommended the marriage of Melisandre to the new earl, asked Eric to make suitable matches for her and Fern the best he could within his daughters' limitations.

Limitations.

Vivian would not have made even this request on their behalf, which was further evidence that he'd penned it. But the fact that he thought so little of her and Fern—something died inside her chest.

Her knees grew weak, and she moved to the settee, sinking down upon it. Eric sat next to her, wrapping his arm about her.

"What's wrong?"

"He didn't..." She didn't even know how to say the words, for the assumption that her father had tried to love her the best he could had been like a thread of hope for so long and that thread had just been cut. "He didn't fight for us at all."

Eric's eyes crinkled as his hand tightened about her. "Didn't fight for you? Are you certain? He was your father."

"These are his words. He asked you to marry Melisandre. Insinuated Fern and I were less, he..."

"Hush." Eric pulled her even closer, lifting her and settling her in his lap. "You don't know that. It could be a forgery."

"It isn't." Something inside her died.

He held her tighter. "He was sick and weak, and he did Vivian's bidding because..."

But she'd stopped listening.

Because her heart ached. She and Fern...they'd had each other for so long, but she'd been a fool to hope that more people would fight for them. That some man would be able to win against Vivian's schemes.

"And Vivian didn't write this. We've proven nothing."

He took the letter from her hand. "Did you notice the date?"

"What about it?"

"It's been blotted out with a large splash of ink." His finger brushed over the spot.

"So?"

"So. She didn't want me to know that the letter was old. I would have rushed here even sooner if I had. She was buying time. I thought it odd when I first noticed the splotch. Men of his station would have rewritten a letter with a stain like this."

But Ella shook her head. Eric was no match for Vivian. And likely, neither was she. But that didn't mean in this one small way, she couldn't thwart Vivian's plans.

There were the shoes...

And then there was the man. Vivian's great plan.

And so she dried her eyes and looked at Eric. "Earlier, you mentioned you wanted to discuss yesterday. What did you wish to say?"

———

ERIC WORKED TIRELESSLY at the books all that day and into the night. He didn't make much progress and knew he ought to ask Ella for help and tell her the whole truth. He could read, enough to make out correspondence and send his own, but the letters danced on the page.

And numbers...they made his eyes cross. But he was winning against Vivian. Or he hoped he was. He'd stopped her plot to marry him to Melisandre, and he'd find the money.

Or he'd hire men who could. But either way, he wanted—he

wished to be Ella's hero in a way her father had not. Some part deep inside him desired to be her rescuer. She was fragile, abused, hurt. He could save her from all that, lift her up and make her life better.

Perhaps then, she wouldn't mind his faults so much...

And he could work on them too, just as he did now. When he'd been young, he'd given up, and as a young man, he'd learned to deflect, deny, distract.

He put on an act as a degenerate rake rather than share the truth.

But if he could save Ella...

They could marry and he could share his weaknesses, knowing that he'd also shown his strength, his worth.

She'd asked him about their kiss...

But he'd only smiled and said she was right. They'd discuss that stolen moment after they'd come up with a plan.

She'd nodded, but she hadn't met his gaze.

Over the past several days, he'd seen the distance that had clouded her expression when they'd first met disappear, clear honesty lighting it instead.

But after she looked at that letter, it was as though all her walls had gone back up and her eyes had shuttered once again.

He tried to imagine what it might be like to have a father who didn't support him. Eric doubted himself constantly, and yet that had been with the love and support of his parents.

But Ella...

Hadn't her father seen how much merit his own daughters had? Their strength, their poise, and their intelligence? How had the man not fought for them?

He ran a frustrated hand through his hair, his gaze landing on the line of neat bottles on the buffet. He'd not dull his pain tonight nor his senses.

And he'd not feed into his image of a fool by drinking too much again.

Rising, he crossed to the window, staring out into the dark. Whatever he'd imagined in coming here to Castleton, this place was so much better and so much worse than in his mind.

His attraction to Ella had him humming with potential, but the situation between the women... Fern and Ella on one side, Vivian and Melisandre on the other.

He shook his head. It was a knot that seemed impossible to untie.

He was the earl—perhaps he should just stuff Vivian in some dowager house while he hired investigators to find the money. Not a bad plan...

What he needed was to move so that he might think. Get out and do something other than sit in this house and stare at books that made no sense. With that in mind, he started outside, making his way down the back stairs and into the night.

Once in the dark, he drew in a cleansing breath, making his way toward the river that he'd bathed in that first night.

He found the rushing water and then followed the bank along the bends until he reached the very spot where he'd stopped to bathe, and he'd first seen Ella under that tree.

She'd been such a delightful mystery, then. And now...well, now she still was. He nearly chuckled out loud, knowing that she was as interesting as she was intelligent and beautiful.

"Needed some air too?"

He'd recognize Ella's voice anywhere and by the slight movement, she was once again under the tree. "What you are you doing out here?"

"Thinking, mostly."

"Thinking?"

"I don't know much about how one might make money disappear, but that hasn't stopped me from trying to figure it out."

He started toward the tree, dipping under the low canopy of branches. The moonlight that filtered through cast down on her where she lounged under the tree, propped on one elbow. She looked like an ethereal figure sent from heaven.

He paused for a moment, just drinking in the sight of her. "You don't find that terribly frustrating? Knowing you'll likely not get it right?" He sat down next to her and stretched out too, propping on an elbow of his own, to face her.

She shrugged. "Sometimes it isn't about winning or losing. I lose against Vivian far more than I win, but I feel better for trying."

His eyes widened a bit as he considered those words. Did he feel better for trying today? The answer was yes. Yes, he did. He felt better for wrestling with those books, and for not turning to a drink when he'd grown frustrated. "I admire that about you."

She leaned closer to him, then, her lips softly parted as she searched his face. "And I admire how strong—"

But he didn't let her finish. Instead, he captured her mouth with his, kissing her, not with a gentle brush but with the fire that was burning inside him. Despite his doubts, Ella had challenged him to do better, and he appreciated that nearly as much as he desired her.

She responded by tilting her head back, opening to him as her arm wrapped about his neck. He pulled her close, the press of her body making him groan, slanting open her mouth, his tongue plundering the sweet depths of her mouth.

The kiss went on and on, her tongue tentatively meeting his in a way that made him growl with satisfaction, and he slid a hand up her back, feeling the curve of her spine, the dip at the small of her back.

He skimmed his hand lower, tracing the curve of her bottom and pulling their pelvises closer.

She gasped into his mouth, her arm tightening about his neck. They were meant to be together like this, and one by one all his doubts fell away.

This woman brought out the best in him. The fighter. The man who tried even when he failed, the man who could persevere.

This was where he belonged. So many of his doubts melted away with the realization that it wasn't just about finding a woman who could do the tasks he could not, it was about working harder on himself and owning up to where he'd failed.

Her fingers curled into his hair, her body still twined about his.

Slowly, he eased back, knowing he should wait until they were engaged. Ella was vulnerable and he needed to be the man who cared for her more than he did his own wants and desires.

Her gaze searched his. "Eric? I...we..."

"I know," he answered, sitting up and pulling her with him. "We desperately need to talk about the future."

"We do."

"We have one," he answered simply. He saw the relief that filled her eyes as she tipped forward, kissing him again.

"I'm so glad."

He was too. Somehow, making the decision made him feel lighter and still stronger. "There is so much I need to tell you about me and I want to share it all."

She shook her head. "I understand. With Vivian's plots hanging over us, it's difficult to really share."

"It is," he answered. "But know that I plan to make you my wife as soon as I've sent her away."

Then he rose, pulling her up. "Now. Let's return to the house before anyone misses us. I don't want any scandal touching you."

"Innocence is always key," she said as she let him lead her back toward the kitchen.

CHAPTER NINE

STEALING the single slipper was easy. Ella stood over the box, looking down at the pair of them neatly nestled amidst the folds of silk. Melisandre was not in her room and Ella had simply slid her hand around the cold glass and slipped one of the shoes into the pocket of the apron she'd tied about her waist. She thought about taking both of them, but one just seemed more insulting.

Ella didn't even want to wear the shoes. She just didn't want Melisandre to have them. She hesitated for a moment, looking at the single shoe in the box, her thoughts drifting to Eric and the kiss they'd just shared.

He'd promised to marry her...

That thought had filled her with both victory and guilt. He was a good man and she'd withheld the truth, manipulated the situation. Once she took this shoe, she'd be declaring war. Wasn't it enough to have his hand? To know that Vivian and Melisandre would be sent away?

But this was a direct cut to Melisandre, the cruel and entitled step-sister who took everything because she thought she deserved it.

Still, much as Ella wanted to make Melisandre hurt, she lost herself every time Eric touched her. She forgot that she wanted revenge, that he might fail her exactly the way her father had, and she just felt his touch without her thoughts racing.

Which was not the plan. She'd almost won this war she'd secretly been waging. She was going to be countess. Later, she could be able to appreciate that Eric was a man she could love, and he might love her in return. Was it possible?

He deserved a good wife, a woman of merit. Once this business was done, she'd be good, and faithful, and honest.

For now, however, what she'd focus on was besting Vivian and Melisandre. And, of course, providing for Fern.

With the slipper in her pocket, she made her way to her room and slowly slid the bed with the narrow frame to the side, then she pried the loose board up, revealing her trove of treasures.

Sliding the slipper among them, she stared at its gleaming surface for a moment before she carefully replaced the board and returned the bed to its usual position.

After hanging up her apron, she smoothed down her skirts and then started for the door. Dinner was about to be served and she was going to enjoy the meal. It didn't matter how little Vivian fed her.

She'd sit there full on the knowledge that she'd won.

———

ERIC HELD HIS CANDLE ALOFT, making his way to the dining room, knowing he was late for dinner.

It was just that thoughts of that kiss had been making his head swirl. Ella had been so lovely in his arms. But also, there were the words he'd not said. He should have told her about his problems then and there. But he was afraid. He could confess that to himself. What if she found him less than?

What if trusting her was a mistake? He wanted to—but there were times she was so open, and then others...

He stopped abruptly as a scream echoed through the house. He spun, charging toward the sound.

Melisandre's screeches followed, her words indiscernible but the tone clear. She was furious about something.

A tantrum, Eric was certain. He set his candle down on a table and trotted toward the front of the house, following the noise.

"She took it, I know she did, and if she doesn't give it back, I'm going to end her!" With each word, Melisandre's voice rose until the threat was made in a high-pitched shriek.

He reached the second-floor landing and looked down at the entry, all four women standing like the points on a compass. Melisandre's face was a purple-red, and in her hand, she held a single glass slipper.

She waved it wildly about, as she drew in hissing gasps of air. "Do you hear me? Give it back or I'll—"

"Melisandre," his voice boomed over the entry. "That is enough."

He cared little if Melisandre was a spoiled princess, until she began threatening others. That, he would not stand, particularly when those threats were aimed at Ella.

The need to protect Ella rose like the tide, swelling and filling his insides as he started down the stairs.

"It is enough," Melisandre shouted back. "I've had enough of Ella's thieving and lying."

Thieving? Lying? His steps slowed as his gaze darted to Ella. He knew she spied on her stepmother and sister in her attempts to be prepared for their plans. But would she steal? His chest tightened. He hoped not. He had plans for their future, but how could he marry a woman who might be a thief, after everything he'd been through. "Those are serious accusations to—"

"She takes my dresses, my hairbrushes, my accessories, and now"— Melisandre waved a slipper about—"she's stolen one of my shoes. One. What am I supposed to do with one shoe?"

"A shoe that did not fit?" Ella asked, not a trace of derision or irritation her voice. "I fail to see—"

"It's mine," Melisandre snarled. "Give it back. Now."

"I don't know what you're talking about," Ella replied, folding her arms over her chest. "What would I want with one—"

But she stopped as Melisandre's arm reared up and then slashed down, the glass slipper flying to the floor and smashing at Ella's feet, glass shards spraying everywhere.

Ella cried out, her hands flinging up to cover her face, bright red spots of blood appearing on her palms.

Every muscle twitched with the need to protect her, spurring Eric forward again as he sprinted in front of Ella, his body blocking hers. Melisandre charged at him, running headlong into his chest, as though to push him away.

He easily and gently subdued her, his voice quiet and low as he issued a single word warning. "Enough."

"But she is a thief," Melisandre shrieked. "You have to punish her. You have to—"

"Melisandre, you will not talk to her that way." The glass breaking had reminded him exactly who was the villain in this situation. "That is my future wife, and you will give her the respect she deserves."

"No," Vivian gasped, coming to her daughter's side. "You can't. I won't allow it."

Melisandre stumbled into her mother's arms, leaving him free to look at Vivian. "The choice was never yours," he said.

Vivian opened her mouth to argue and then raised her hand, bringing it across his cheek with a loud crack that filled the entry.

He'd never hit a woman, not that he wasn't tempted in this moment, but he stood taller and looked down at her, allowing all his contempt to fill his gaze. "Are you done?"

"No," she snarled. "Not even close."

"I beg to differ." He pointed his finger. "Trays will be brought to your rooms. Tomorrow morning at eight sharp, you are to report to my study, where we will discuss where you'll be going."

"Going?" Melisandre sobbed. "What does he mean, Mother?"

But Vivian had drawn herself up, her gaze growing calculating as she stared back at Eric. "Eight sounds perfect. I look forward to it, in fact. We'll have a great deal to discuss."

Then, chin high, she turned and walked away. Unease still sat in his stomach. Somehow, Eric got the feeling that had not been the victory he'd hoped it would be.

CHAPTER TEN

ELLA LOOKED into Eric's gaze, her insides churning, her hands and wrists stinging from all the cuts. Melisandre always grew angry when Ella taunted her, but she'd never been violent before.

But the concern in Eric's eyes made her stomach twist. In part, she'd goaded that behavior out of Melisandre. She wasn't exactly an innocent party, and his worry wasn't completely unjustified.

She deserved some of it, most of it—though Melisandre deserved her tricks too. But then again...how did that make her better than her stepfamily?

Ought she rise above?

Fern's words came back to her. Eric had it in his power to save them. And while he might not be able to outmaneuver Vivian, he was successfully strong-arming her, pushing her into a weaker and weaker position in the house, and now he was going to send Vivian and Melisandre away.

He'd stood so tall in front of her, protecting her, defending her, and then declaring that Vivian was leaving. He'd done so much more for her than anyone else had in such a long time.

And what had she done? She'd largely ignored his help as she attempted to gain her petty revenge.

It was just that her father's words had hurt so much. And they'd made her feel like her own little games were the only sure-fire defense.

She hadn't always been like this, but since her father's death, she'd been furious with the position in which he'd left them to rot. And something in her had shifted. Before he'd passed, she'd held some hope that her father would realize Vivian's heart and take care of his daughters again. But after seeing that letter, she'd known the truth...he would never have been able to see the light and save them.

And she'd assumed Eric wouldn't either...

"Ella?" he asked, gently taking her wrist in his hand. "Are you all right?"

Tears clogged her throat. Not from the cuts, but simply...everything. "I'm fine. I'll be fine."

"Let's get you cleaned up," he said as his other hand came to her waist. "Fern, would you help me?"

"Of course," her sister answered with a nod. But her gaze cut to Ella's and her eyes widened, her mouth thinning. She knew what Fern was attempting to say. *Why did you take that shoe?*

He started leading her toward the kitchen. "Melisandre will answer for how she hurt you," Eric assured her, his hand spread wide on her back. "I promise you that."

"Thank you," she croaked out, guilt still making her feel heavy as he helped her toward the kitchen.

"Why would she think that you'd taken the slipper?"

"I don't..."

"Ahem," Fern said behind them, coughing loudly.

Did her sister wish for her to tell the truth? That she'd been enacting her own little revenge schemes? That she'd planned a much larger scheme to steal him?

But that kiss hadn't felt like stealing, it had been far more like falling...

Her breath caught as her gaze slid to him, so tall and strong next to her. If the wasn't careful, this man could capture her heart.

He was just so good. Decent and honest, strong and caring. Her breath hitched, knowing she wasn't nearly good enough for him.

Her life had been so ugly for so long, and when she'd lost her father, she'd allowed that ugliness to fill her, move her.

She choked on the thoughts, her lungs constricting. Fern had told her she was crossing a line from defense to revenge, but she'd been so angry.

"They're leaving tomorrow," Eric was saying. "There is a dowager house, surely, that we can send her to. Or another property in the far north? Somewhere they can't do any more damage. I'll have to make certain to send her with a footman who will actually see her to the destination. Mine, perhaps. The ones here are likely loyal to her."

She heard Fern's gasp, and she looked over her shoulder to see her sister's eyes were so big, they threatened to fall out of her head. "Send them away?" Fern asked, her eyes filling with a hope that Ella hadn't seen in months. Inwardly, she winced again. Why hadn't Ella trusted this man sooner?

Eric nodded. "I'll keep watch on them. Hire investigators to find that money. Surely someone will work on the promise of payment upon completion of the job. I've seen enough to know they've done something terrible, and I'll not live with vipers under my roof."

More doubts swelled from her stomach to her chest. Vipers under his roof. What would he think of her?

They entered the kitchen, and he sat her on a stool. "I'm just going to get water to clean those cuts. I'll be right back."

He disappeared into the next room to access the well, and Fern spun to her with a hissing breath. "Tell him."

"Tell him what?" she whispered back, already knowing.

"Everything." Fern stomped her foot. "We're so close, Ella. Tell him."

"But." She shook her head. "What if he casts me out too? What if he hates me after what I..." Telling him the truth was such a risk. The possibilities made her head spin.

"He won't," Fern whispered back, placing a hand on her shoulder. "But you need to be honest. You can't build anything on lies, and he's got enough mistrust and manipulation fighting with Vivian. You heard him. He's hiring men to guard her and investigators to find what she's stolen. Help him. Don't deceive him."

Those words rang with a truth that stole her breath. "The truth... Fern." She drew in a ragged breath. "I'm sorry if I've ruined everything. I never—"

Fern shook her head. "It isn't ruined. Not yet."

"But what if it is?"

Fern gave her a rare smile. "Then we'll find another way. We always do."

In that moment, love for her sister overwhelmed her. She'd started stealing to protect her sister. That had been noble in its own way and she could justify actions done out of love. She had to focus on that.

Eric came back, dumping the bucket of water into a pot on the stove.

Then he began to clean the wounds, first with cold water and then again with hot, carefully wrapping her hands with clean cloth.

Fern kept her hand on Ella's shoulder as he worked, the silence stretching between the three of them. And the longer Ella sat with Fern's words, the more she knew they were true. She did need to tell him all of it. How her father's betrayal had made her so hurt, how she'd planned to steal his hand in order to best Vivian, but also how—

How he'd managed to claim her heart.

He finished wrapping the wounds and his hand rose to her cheek. "I'd like for you and Fern to sleep in the room next to mine," he said, his fingertips lightly caressing her. "I don't want to take any chances that there will be any more violence tonight. And if you're far away from me..."

Fern's hand tightened on her shoulder.

Ella wanted to tell him everything, but she needed privacy for the chance to explain. "All right."

"Good," he said and then he slid his hand down her neck. "I need to know you're safe."

"Thank you," she said, biting at her lips as she looked up at him.

Was Fern right? Would he forgive her, or would the truth rip apart the tentative bond they'd formed?

———

Eric settled Fern and Ella into the room that connected to his, his blood boiling with carefully controlled fury.

How dare Melisandre hurt Ella like that? He'd known that she was a selfish person, but to be so violent...

He started back to his study, determined to choose a property where he could banish Vivian and Melisandre. One in his viscountcy might do the trick. It was fully staffed with people who were loyal to him. He had a nice, small house in the north. Old and a bit run down, but thousands of acres around it.

It was perfect.

He rounded the corner, intent upon writing the letter that would start the process, when he found Vivian in his study.

He stopped in the door. "I thought we agreed you'd remain in your room for the night."

"And I thought you ordered me to do so, but as I have not taken orders for a very long time..."

"You only give them?" He crossed his arms over his chest. "Like whom I ought to marry."

Vivian's chin notched up at a regal angle. "I'm not wrong."

"I beg to differ."

He opened his mouth to tell her to get out of his study when she held up her hands. "What if I could prove it to you?"

"Prove what?"

Vivian drew herself up. "I'm going to prove to you that Ella is not the hapless victim here and that you have been misled."

Melisandre's hurtled accusations ran through his thoughts as he remained exactly where he was standing. "You will return to your room while I decide where I am going to send you and Melisandre. And what's more, you won't leave because you are grateful that I have not yet involved a constable in the matter."

"Constable?"

"I don't know what sort of man you took me for, perhaps one like your former husband, but my word alone will send you to prison."

He saw her pale then, doubt darkening her eyes. "You wouldn't."

"I'd prefer not to bring that sort of scandal to any of us, which is why I expect you to do as I have asked."

He stepped out of the doorway then, sweeping his hand toward the hall as a silent command for her to leave.

She did, managing to keep her chin up, but her eyes held a wild sort of light that he'd never seen before.

He understood. He'd trapped her in a corner. He'd not play her games, he'd not take her bait, and he would prove her wrongdoing. With help, of course.

She stopped in front him, the hard line of her mouth pressing thinner. "If you want to know the truth, just go to Ella's room. You will learn all you need to know there."

He didn't respond, his jaw hardening. He watched her disappear down the hall as he continued to stand in the doorway.

But he didn't step into his office, either. What did Vivian mean and what might he find if he did as she'd requested and looked in Ella's room?

CHAPTER ELEVEN

ELLA WOKE to the first rays of the sun. Despite the ache in her hands, she'd slept fitfully for much of the night.

Knowing that Vivian was leaving, that this was nearly over, had caused a peace to settle over her that she hadn't experienced in months.

Fern being next to her had helped too. In the early days after their mother's death, they'd slept together often, holding one another as they'd cried.

That was before they'd each built their armor, and she hoped that with better times, they'd begin to remove some of the carefully constructed barriers that had come up around them, even with each other.

She loved Fern. Always had. But it was difficult to give to anyone emotionally after what they'd been through.

Perhaps that was why it had been so tough to trust in Eric as well. But it was time to correct that.

She rose from the bed, pulling on a dressing gown, moving to the dressing table. It had been a long time since she'd slept in a room this fine, and she glanced about the ornate trim work and the shell-pink paint.

This had been her mother's room and it had been the one line that her father had drawn. Vivian had never occupied this space.

Perhaps that's why she'd hoped that her father might stand up for them too.

A soft knock sounded at the door. She looked at Fern, who still lay sleeping, and crossed the room. "Who is it?"

"It's me," came Eric's soft whisper. "I need to speak with you."

She opened the door, glad for a moment of privacy. She had so much to say, so much to share...

But the look on his face made the words die on her lips. His mouth was pinched in a tight line, his eyes hard and unreadable.

She stepped out, closing the door. "What's wrong?"

"Follow me," was his only answer as he started down the hall. She followed behind him, keenly aware that he did not have a hand at her waist.

She wanted to ask more. Had something happened? But her lips refused to work, and when he started up the stairs to the third floor, her stomach sank. That was where her room was located.

Not her old one that Melisandre had stolen, but her tiny room with its bare wooden walls and narrow bed. The door was open, and she paused for a moment, her hand coming up to her throat as she swallowed down a lump of dread. "Eric."

He didn't stop until he'd reached the doorway. Then he looked back at her, his features harder than ever.

She already knew what he'd found and why she was here.

Her head bowed down in shame. "I'm sorry."

His shoulders seemed to deflate with her words. "I thought maybe you'd deny it. That you'd say Vivian planted it."

Drawing in a trembling breath, she moved past him into the room. The bed had been pushed to the side, the board removed from her hiding spot. In it was the slipper, winking up at her, as well as several other items covered in various amounts of dust. "It's pointless, and besides," she said, her throat constricting, "I won't lie to you."

"Going forward?" he asked. "You won't lie to me going forward?"

Those words made her breath catch with fear. "I haven't been

78

honest in all of my intentions, and I've omitted several details, but I've not lied."

His eyes widened and then grew distant, and she knew he was recalling several conversations they'd shared.

"I…" She pulled herself up straighter. "I can't justify my actions, but I can tell you this. I haven't been able to rely on anyone in so long…I forgot how."

Surprise filled his eyes, and he took a step closer. "I see."

"I know it doesn't justify me stealing that slipper. For the longest time, I only stole what Fern and I really needed. Food. Fabric to keep us warm. She was so little and…" Her breath caught at the memories. "But when my father grew ill, I just couldn't seem to control the hate that pulsed through me. I wanted revenge."

She looked at him, hoping to see some spark of understanding, some softening. His eyes were closed, fine lines spidering out around them. "I haven't shared everything about myself, either."

Those words gave her a bit of hope. Did he understand? "Tell me now." She took a step toward him, one of her hands lifting.

"I can't understand the ledgers."

"What?" She didn't know what she'd expected, but that hadn't been it.

"My entire life, I tried. Studied. Worked at them. I'm not great with letters, either, but I can at least read and write. But numbers…" He ran a hand through his hair, his movements jerky and agitated. "They dance about the page. I can't hold them in my head."

She shook her head, feeling his frustration. "Oh, Eric. There are so many people who can do that for you. You needn't—"

"My last accountant stole massive sums from me. Under investigation now. I'll likely use the same men to find out what Vivian has done."

She stopped, her hand dropping as his eyes opened, his gaze catching and holding hers. She's hoped for some softness in them, but they were blank. Unreadable.

"That…is a good idea." Her hands pressed to her stomach.

"But a man I trusted used my weakness to hurt my viscountcy."

Her breath held in her lungs for so long they began to burn, because she suddenly she understood. "You think I might do that to you?"

"I don't know." He shook his head. "But I know your actions have cast doubt and I—" He stopped.

She brought a shaking hand to her mouth, her knees weak. Not knowing what else to do, she sat on the bed. "Fern is blameless."

"What?"

Her hand dropped as her back straightened. "Fern did nothing to help me in this plot. In fact, she tried to stop me."

"This is what you two were arguing about."

"Yes," she nodded. "But whatever you do to me, please, don't punish her. She deserves a good life with a kind man after everything Vivian has done to her." Tears she didn't want to shed rose in her eyes.

He stared at her with his lips parted, studying her. "Ella. I know you've been backed into a corner, and I know why you did what you did. I even know why you met me at the river that first day. You wanted to steal me too."

She trembled at the harsh truth of it. That she'd been that transparent. "I didn't know you then. I didn't—"

"But you do now, which is why you should know I would never punish you for trying to fight your way out the corner Vivian pushed you into. It's just that my own weaknesses..." He waved a hand uselessly. "I need to think. And you should eat. It's going to be a busy day seeing off Vivian and Melisandre."

A bubble of hope rose inside her. "You're still sending them away?"

"Of course I am," he answered with the first ghost of a smile.

He started to turn but suddenly she was on her feet, and she raced to his side, touching his arm. "Eric."

He looked at her again, his gaze a bit sad in a way that made her ache. "Yes?"

"I'm sorry." The words tumbled like water from her lips. "I was wrong. I wanted revenge, I did, and I didn't know how to trust you after all that had happened."

His hand came to her waist. She wanted to press into that comfort, into his warmth. "I understand."

Her eyes fluttered closed as her lips trembled around the words. "And I'm not sure I deserve a man like you, but I want you to know something."

"What?"

"I heard in your voice that you're angry at yourself for not being able to read those ledgers."

"I am."

"But I say that you are the best man I ever met and if anyone deserves to be happy, to be fulfilled, to love themselves, it's you." And then she rose on tiptoe and kissed his cheek. "If you don't wish to marry me, I will release you without a word, but I want you to know that the woman who gets you is not getting something broken or defective. She is getting a man deserving of the deepest love."

And then she let him go, and not able to hold back her tears any longer, she sprinted from the room. It would hurt too much to look in his eyes and see the sadness of goodbye.

———

ERIC STARTED AFTER ELLA, her words breaking some shell that he'd been fortifying around his heart.

He had always understood her actions. She'd been locked in battle with her stepmother and stepsister. Hell, he'd been taken advantage of once and he was scarred.

She'd been abused over and over.

And yet...she'd still found it in her heart to tell him that she thought him a good man. The best.

Had he done the same for her? Told her that he'd love her despite her failings? Pain lanced through his chest.

He started down the stairs, not even certain what he'd say. But he needed to say something. He couldn't leave her thinking that he didn't care.

But he was waylaid on the second floor when the butler appeared before him. "Your solicitor is here."

"Already?" Had the man left the instant he'd received the missive? What had he learned to send him here so quickly? "Show him to my study."

He looked down the hall, trying to spot Ella, but he couldn't see her. With a grunt of frustration, he started toward his study, sure that he could find Ella as soon as this meeting was done.

Mr. Henshaw was shown in moments later, the look of relief on the man's face making Eric stop his own pacing. The other man adjusted the thin-rimmed spectacles that were always perched upon his nose and he gave Eric a short bow.

Eric normally never skipped the niceties, but too much had happened. "Mister Henshaw. Good to see you. What did you find out about Lady Sanbridge?"

"Lady Sanbridge?" the man asked, stopping in his tracks. "What do you mean, my lord?"

He stared at Henshaw, trying to decide what had just gone wrong. "Did you not come here in response to my letter?"

"I did not." He shook his head. "I came to personally deliver the news that your accountant has been found and a great deal of your money recovered."

His mouth hung open for a moment as he blinked at the man. "You're serious?"

"I am. The investigators you hired have proved valuable indeed."

"That is excellent news." Relief washed through him, and letting out a rush of air, he sat on the settee. "Please, Mister Henshaw, would you care to sit?"

The man sank down into a chair. "Now, my lord, perhaps you should tell me what correspondence you expected me to be here addressing."

In short order, Eric told Mr. Henshaw all that he knew about Vivian and the treachery at work in the house, from the books to the poor state of the earl's two daughters. He left out any details about Ella and the shoes.

But Henshaw's thoughtful gaze prompted Eric to show him the ledger with all the missing columns.

Mr. Henshaw made quick work of reviewing them and then straightened. "There is no hard proof in these ledgers, but it's enough to hire the investigators, I think."

"So do I."

"And what will you do with the countess in the meantime?"

"I've got a home I can send her to, make sure she's safe but unable to cause any more trouble."

Mr. Henshaw gave a quick nod. "It shouldn't take the investigators long. This sort of treachery is beyond my knowledge, but they seem well versed."

"Thank you," he said as he crossed the room and rang the bell. "Let me set up a room for you and order a tray of breakfast sent. I'm sure you're tired after your journey."

Mr. Henshaw shook his head. "If it's all the same to you, we ought to eat here and begin sending the necessary letters. It's a matter best dealt with quickly, I should think."

Eric smiled, grateful for Mr. Henshaw's quick attention to the matter. Though part of him still wished to be with Ella. He hated the way they'd left things. And she'd want to know what had just transpired.

But Mr. Henshaw was right. This was important and he'd be able to speak with her soon enough.

CHAPTER TWELVE

ELLA DRESSED, her movements so automatic that she was hardly aware of them. She'd woken with such hope...

But after her confrontation with Eric, all that optimism was gone. Fern had been right all along. She caught her sister's gaze in the mirror, cringing as she shook her head.

"It was awful, Fern." She sat down at the vanity, her chin sinking to her chest.

Fern came up behind her and unplaited Ella's long blonde hair. Then with the horsehair brush, she brushed out the thick locks. "It's all right, I'm sure of it. He didn't say he was ending the engagement, just that he needed to think."

"I know, but..."

Fern's touch was so gentle as she smoothed the strands. "And what you said to him at the end, that was wonderful."

Ella had come back to the room, confessing all that had happened to her sister. She leaned her head back, turning it to the side so that her cheek pressed to her sister's stomach. "I failed you, I failed myself, and I definitely failed him."

"No." Fern's voice held a firmness that made Ella sit up straight again. "You saved him."

"I didn't." She shook her head in denial.

"You discovered the discrepancy in the books that has allowed him to send Vivian and Melisandre away. You've shielded me all these years, and you take on the fight, so I don't have to."

Suddenly Fern's arms were around her. "I love you."

Emotion overwhelmed her. "I love you too."

"And don't you dare tell a soul that we hugged." But Fern squeezed her all the tighter.

That made Emma laugh, at least a little. Whatever else happened, she could say one good thing had come from all this...she and Fern hadn't spoken like this in ages. "Your secret is safe with me."

"Now." Fern began twisting up her sister's hair. "We're going to go to breakfast and we're going to sit in that dining room like the victors we are."

"You don't think that Vivian and Melisandre would dare come to breakfast after last night?"

"You never know with the two of them." Fern's mouth pinched as she finished pinning the strands. "All that matters though is the future. Once Vivian and Melisandre are gone, we'll find a way to convince Eric that you deserve a second chance."

Ella had never been more grateful for Fern than she was in this moment. Her sister placed her hands on both of Ella's shoulders, giving her a long look in the mirror. "If anyone can convince him to marry, it's you. I'm sure of it."

Ella rose, so grateful for her sister's words, the two of them walking arm and arm to breakfast.

Ella shouldn't have been surprised, but she started at the sight of Vivian and Melisandre sitting at their usual spots at the table. She made a mental note to listen to Fern far more often.

"Good morning." Vivian gave them a smooth smile that immediately set Ella's teeth on edge. She'd seen the cold, calculating look many times before, but it still sent a shiver running down her spine.

"Good morning," she replied, crossing to the buffet and putting eggs and sausage on her plate. Whatever was coming would surely require real fortification on her part. Even in the week that Eric had been here, she'd seen some of the hollows in her face smoothing out and she'd not let Vivian undo Eric's good. Fern joined her, silently glaring about the room.

She returned to the table just as one of the maids set a steaming teapot in front of her. Her gaze flicked to the woman she didn't recognize. When had she joined the staff? Then again, Ella rarely attended breakfast, but on the rare occasion she did, she was never served anything. Was this woman just so new, she didn't understand?

Vivian tilted her chin up. "A sign of your new status?"

Ella didn't answer as she poured the steaming liquid into her teacup, taking several bites of her eggs before she lifted the cup and took a drink.

The hot liquid slid down her throat, soothing the scratchiness from her earlier tears and fortifying her strength. "Did the earl not ask you to stay in your rooms?"

"We're not allowed to eat?" Melisandre harrumphed as she also took a bite of her toast.

Vivian's hand came out to touch her daughter's arm. "Now, now. There is no need for that. We are family, after all."

Ella took another sip of her tea. "Family. Right." But her head gave the strangest spin. She lifted her fingers to her temple.

"Are you all right?" Fern asked, breaking her usual silence.

Ella started to sway in her chair, or perhaps the floor was tipping.

"Drink your tea, dear. It will help," Vivian called from the other end of the table. "Trust me."

"Trust you?" But the words came out garbled and strange.

"I'm getting his lordship," Fern said, jumping from her chair and racing from the room.

Ella wanted to call her back. *Don't leave me with them.* But she couldn't seem to get the words out of her head and into her mouth.

Darkness started to close in her vision and then she was falling out of the chair and onto the thick carpet that adjoined the floor.

"Will it be quick?" Melisandre asked.

"Quicker than her father, I hope. I had to dose him slowly."

Dose him? But she couldn't ask, with the world closing to darkness.

———

ERIC WATCHED as Mr. Henshaw penned letter after letter, the quill flying over the pages with a dizzying speed.

Eric could write, but his work was slow and methodical. Same with his reading. He had to really concentrate, or the letters seemed to go backwards in his mind.

As the man worked, he asked Eric questions. "How long since the husband died?"

"Three months."

"What were the symptoms?"

"I'd have to ask Ella." Ella. His chest ached. "She'll be able to give you a detailed accounting."

"Would you mind if I spoke with her now? I'd like to give the investigators as much information as possible before they've even arrived."

"Of course." He pushed off the mantel he'd been leaning on and started for the door. But he hadn't made it across the room when the door flew open, Fern's fear-filled gaze meeting his. "Ella," she gasped. "Come quickly."

"What's wrong?" he asked, but he was already closing the distance between them, his hand slipping into Fern's as she pulled him out of the study and down the hall.

"She isn't well. She was fine one minute, drinking her tea and eating her eggs, and the next—"

"The next?" Fear pulsed through his body, roaring in his ears.

From behind him, Mr. Henshaw asked, "Not well how?"

Fern looked at him, the question shining in her eyes. He gave a quick nod.

"She became very dizzy and pale."

"Ella's already pale."

"Deathly pale," Fern said, voice breaking into a sob. "Please, my lord."

"Eric," he said, squeezing her fingers. "And tell me everything."

Fern began detailing Vivian, Melisandre, the maid, and the tea.

Behind them, Mr. Henshaw cleared his throat. "Could be arsenic."

Eric screeched to a halt. "What?"

"It's a bit of a problem, actually. They're legislating the substance, but after all I've heard, I wouldn't rule out poisoning."

Poison? He let go of Fern's hand and broke into a full run, his heart nearly bursting from his chest as he entered the dining room to find Ella on the floor. No one else was in the room, another sign that Vivian had had something to do with whatever happened. He wrapped Ella in his coat and then hefted her into his arms.

"What are you doing?" Fern gasped.

"It will be faster if I take her to the doctor." Then he started back out the door. "If you would like to retain your position in this house, I want my carriage now!" his voice boomed out to no one in particular as he ran with Ella in his arms.

When he got back, he'd take a full accounting from every staff member.

Mr. Henshaw was still on his heels. "I'll watch over Lady Fern," he said, adjusting his spectacles.

"Thank you," he answered, grateful to the man as he swept through the front door.

Miraculously, the carriage waited for him, and a footman snapped the door open. He stepped inside in one sweeping movement, the door snapping shut behind him. The whip crack rent the air and he'd hardly sat before the carriage began to roll, heading toward the village.

Ella moaned softly in his arms, and he pulled her closer, his eyes squeezing shut. This entire time, she'd been in a fight for her very life. He'd promised to protect her...

His stomach twisted. He'd failed. Ella had been right not to trust him, because he'd had no idea of what Vivian was capable of.

He stroked her hair back, her skin so sallow that fear beat like a drum in his chest. He'd been so worried about how her behavior might affect him that he'd forgotten that he was the real problem. Everything he touched fell apart in his hands.

"Please, Ella," he begged. "Please be all right. I'll do whatever it takes to be the man you need. I swear it. Just give me that chance."

She moaned again, her lashes fluttering.

His breath held in his lungs. Ella was strong. Tough. Tougher than anyone he'd ever known. Surely, she had a chance of fighting this. "Ella? Love?"

"Eric?" she croaked, fluttering her hand. "My stomach."

"I know, love." He held her tighter. "We're going to the doctor."

"You'll save me."

He choked on his own emotions. How could she have faith in him now? He'd allowed this—

But this was the moment where he couldn't allow self-doubt to choke him. This was the moment where he was the man she needed him to be.

"I will save you, sweetheart."

The carriage began to slow, and he reached over, snapping the door open. He didn't wait for the carriage to stop as he jumped out and broke into a run again.

The doctor had better be in...

CHAPTER THIRTEEN

ELLA CAME in and out of wakefulness, catching words and phrases but not really understanding them.

She finally woke, darkness around her. Where was she? "Hello?" Her voice sounded scratchy even to her own ears.

"Ella?" Despite her lips being dry and cracked, she gave a small smile as Eric's deep baritone filled her ears.

"You're here."

"I'm here, my love." His hand slipped into hers for just a moment, lightly squeezing her fingers. "You must be thirsty." And then he reached under her head, a cool glass coming to her lips. The water was sweet and fresh, and it slid down her throat, soothing the soreness. "More?"

"Yes," she answered, taking several swallows.

"How about some broth?" he asked, his voice achingly gentle.

She gave a quick nod. "Yes, please." Warm broth sounded divine, her body aching and sore as she lay back down on the pillow.

He left the room, her eyes adjusting to the dim light. The small room was unfamiliar and she searched about, looking for some clue. The furniture was simple and the walls bare, but the blankets were warm and comfortable about her body.

Eric returned, a bowl in hand.

"Where am I?"

"Doctor Burton's home," he answered. "He was kind enough to allow you to stay so that he might care for you while you recovered."

And then he brought the bowl to her lips. The hot liquid was even better than the cool, the broth not only soothing but bringing some measure of strength with each sip she took. "How long have I been here?"

He brushed back her hair. "Two days."

"Two days?" she gasped, trying to sit up. With a light hand, he easily held her down. "But Vivian—"

"Gone," he answered with a grimace. "I have both investigators and constables searching for her."

"Constables?" Ella asked, studying Eric's tense features for answers. But slowly, Vivian's words and actions began to filter back to her. And then she remembered what her stepmother had said just before she'd lost her senses. "She poisoned me."

"She did."

"And my father too," Ella croaked. "I heard her say so just as I fell to the floor." She shuddered with the knowledge. Why would her stepmother have done such a thing? A new earl was a risk and her father had been under his wife's thumb for such a long time.

"I know."

"You know?"

He gave a nod. "Or I suspect. The investigation has already begun, and it turns out that money has been disappearing for a very long time. About four months ago, there was a flurry of activity in the accounts in your father's handwriting where he seemed to attempt to reconcile the books. He couldn't."

"But the letter. He wrote it. He recommended Melisandre to you and..."

Eric brought the bowl to her mouth again. "I can't answer that for certain, but if I were to guess, he was either very weak or being blackmailed by her to write the letter."

Those words filled her with more comfort than she'd ever imagined. She lifted a hand to him, surprised by how heavy her arm felt.

He grasped her fingers in his and brought them the rest of the way to his lips.

"Do you really think that he was forced to say those things?" she asked, hope filling her chest.

"I do." He leaned down, kissing her forehead. "Now drink the rest of this broth and then we're going to bring you home. A nice bath and good food will help you recover faster than anything else."

She gave a nod, very much wishing to return home. For the first time in a long time, Castleton would be a home again. "How is Fern?"

"She's fine. She'll be very relieved to see you, though." He ran a knuckle down her face to her jaw line. "She's been worried."

"I think it was the tea," she said, knowing that she hardly made sense, jumping from one topic to the next.

Eric didn't seem to mind. "Yes. The doctor had the liquid tested. It was the tea. The saving grace was that you didn't drink much of it because Vivian had put enough in the cup—" He stopped, squeezing her hand again.

"It's all right. Nothing would surprise me at this point."

"It surprised me," he said, his voice rough. "I understand why you didn't trust me to fight for you. I had no idea..." His eyes squeezed closed.

The sun was slowly rising, the room growing brighter. "Eric." She shook her head. "Don't do that. This was not your shortcoming. It was mine. I wanted revenge so badly."

"Everything I've touched has fallen apart in my hands, Ella. I failed you."

"Stop." She shook her head. "My father failed us. You saved me. Never forget that." Eric had rushed her to the doctor, fought Vivian, chosen Ella over Melisandre. She sank her head back down, already a little tired. "We've both made mistakes, but we're going to learn from them. Be better people for them." *If it wasn't too late.*

"I love you," he whispered, his dark eyes holding hers captive.

Her breath caught. Perhaps it wasn't too late... "I love you too."

He kissed the back of her hand again and then he turned, beginning to collect several items about the room. "I'll wake the doctor in just a bit and send for the carriage. We'll get you home while you still have the strength for the short trip."

She wanted to ask more. Did his admission of love mean that they'd wed? Had he forgiven her?

But she didn't ask as he left the room and then came back with the doctor close behind. She'd ask him in the carriage or later today. Perhaps it was best to wait until she had the energy to face whatever his answer might be.

ERIC DID LITTLE for the next three days besides sit at Ella's side. He did bring ledgers with him, and as her strength grew, she answered his questions with a kind patience that both humbled him and filled him with joy. He couldn't say he was getting better at reading the numbers on the page, but he'd learned something from Ella—it was the trying that mattered.

And he'd begun to think of all his failures. How many of them had he just assumed he'd fail and then stopped even attempting to work at them? Covered them up? Hidden away from them?

Ella thought him a good man, but he knew he could be better. Would be better. If Ella could face the adversity she had and still keep fighting, then he could too.

Would he be the man she deserved if he learned to stand up and fight for what he desired?

Ella woke from a nap as the afternoon sun streamed into the windows. She'd been eating well and moving about, but tired quickly, and he'd insisted that she rest.

He looked at her now, her hair plaited over one shoulder while she stretched in the bed, sitting up. "Tell me we can go for a walk this evening. I'm tired of being in bed."

"Hello to you too," he said with a smile, standing so that he might lean down and kiss her forehead.

Her scent wrapped about him, a mix of natural floral tones and the lilac soap she'd used in her bath this morning.

"So. Can we?" she said, pulling the covers off her body. "I'm ready to move and I'm tired of being still."

"Always a fighter," he said with a smile, but she winced, her chin dropping.

Did she think that bad? "I don't mean to be."

He took her hand in his, helping her from the bed. Over the past few days, he'd cared for her a great deal and he'd grown accustomed to touching her, holding her, so it didn't feel odd to pull her close even though she wore only a chemise. "I think it's a wonderful quality."

"Until my tenacity lands me in a plot that threatens someone's life," she said, her head turned away from him. "Most namely my own."

He gently touched her chin, guiding her face to look at his again. "Your willingness to keep pushing forward is a testament to your strength and I admire it greatly."

"But not my willingness to take what isn't mine."

He could see the pain in her eyes. He'd known this conversation was coming. He'd left their relationship on tenuous terms just before Vivian had attempted to kill her and he'd avoided the topic because she'd been so weak.

"Ella," he said, letting out a long breath. "Get dressed. I'm going to have a picnic prepared and then you and I are going to sit under the tree by the river, eat, and talk."

She gave a tentative nod, but worry lines pulled at her eyes and mouth. He sighed, not wanting to worry her but also not wishing to say what he needed to without proper explanation.

He left, making his way to the kitchen, and then returned to her room to find her dressed and ready in a simple gown of sturdy cotton.

He needed to get both her and Fern new wardrobes. Their clothing was lacking.

Holding out his elbow, they started toward the kitchen, where he collected the basket and then they began the short walk to the river. The exercise and fresh air returned some color to her cheeks, and he smiled over at her, glad to see her looking so well. She'd lost whatever weight she'd put on, but he was determined to see her recovered soon enough.

Silence had fallen between them, and he pulled her a touch closer as they walked. "Ella."

"Yes," she said, nibbling at her lip. "I..." She stopped, looking at him. "I thought I was ready for this conversation, but I'm not certain I am."

"What happened to the fearless woman I met?"

"She was poisoned," Ella answered and then shook her head.

"That's not funny," he said with a scowl.

"I'm not sure I was joking." Her large blue eyes lifted to his, the depths of them pleading. "If you don't want me, send me away. Please. I can't stay here and watch you marry someone else. I—"

"Send you away?" He set down the basket and pulled her to him. "Ella. I love you. I told you so."

"I love you too, but after what I did..."

He shook his head. "You were fighting to survive. I see that now. And besides, all the events that transpired were half my fault. A man without my deficits would not have taken such issue with what you did."

"It's not a deficit." She shook her head. "Or at least, it's a normal deficit. We all have one." She placed a hand on his chest, needing him to understand. "You saw me from the beginning, though. I know you did. You saw Vivian too when so many are fooled by her outward charm. That's a skill most lack. How can you not see that you're talented in all your own ways?"

"You think that?" His chest swelled. This was the first time that she'd told him how much she admired him. He appreciated her words more than he knew how to say.

"I do," she answered, giving him a long, unblinking stare. "You're a wonderful man."

"This is why I love you," he said and then his mouth covered hers. The kiss was light and gentle. Eric didn't want to hurt her while she still recovered, but underneath, tension pulsed through him like a current of water, pulling him under.

He settled her body closer, sliding his hands up and down her back as he slanted her lips open, his tongue sweeping against hers.

She twined her fingers into his hair, pulling him closer to answer the sweep of his tongue with one of her own.

His groaned into her mouth, his fingers splaying out on her back, wrapping her deeper into his embrace.

Exactly where she belonged. He needed to stop kissing her long enough to explain the rest...

CHAPTER FOURTEEN

ELLA HAD NEVER WANTED anything more in her life than she wanted this man in this moment. His lips, the press of his body, the feel of his hands.

Considering the circumstances of the past few years and the evilness of her stepmother, saying that she wanted Eric more than she'd wanted revenge was a statement of epic proportion.

When his tongue swept against hers, she met the thrust with one of her own, arching into him. Had she been tired? Worried?

All of that melted away in his embrace, her body humming with such wonderful energy that she wasn't certain where it all came from or where it might go.

She unthreaded her fingers from his hair to skim her fingertips over the skin of his neck. She liked the feel so much that she plucked at the neck cloth, hoping to loosen it so she might feel more of his skin.

He chuckled against her lips, pulling back from the kiss and easing away.

Her brow knitted. "Why are you stopping?"

"Because," he said as he grazed a thumb over her cheek, "we're not done talking and I am only a man, and not even a particularly moral one, and you are very beautiful and incredibly desirable."

A warm wave of pleasure washed over her. "You find me beautiful and desirable?"

"I do," he answered, kissing at the corner of her mouth. "Which is why I am most certainly not sending you away."

"Oh," she breathed, pleasure pulsing through her. "What will you do with me then?"

He kissed a trail over her jaw and down her throat, stopping at the neckline of her gown. "Ella," he said and his voice grew more serious, belying the kisses he was showering her with. "If you'll have me, I mean to marry you."

"If I'll have you?" she asked, leaning back and taking his face in her hands. "I can hardly think of anything else."

"So that's a yes? You'll marry me?"

"Yes," she whispered. "Yes, I'll marry you."

"Even knowing my failings?"

She gave a nod. "Just as you know mine."

He picked her up by the waist, spinning her in the air before he lightly set her on her feet again. "In that case, I won't feel the least bit guilty in kissing you again."

"Don't," she whispered, more excitement pulsing through her. "Kiss me," she murmured against his lips. "Don't ever stop."

But those words had the opposite of the intended effect. He leaned back, his gaze searching hers.

"Eric?"

He bent down and picked up the basket with one hand and then wrapped his other arm under her behind before lifting her into the air. She gave a little shriek of surprise as she steadied herself on his shoulders.

He chuckled. "Steady, sweetheart."

She curled her upper body around him, resting her cheek on the top of head. Steady. She'd never been more so than she was now. Fern would be proud. Ella understood that revenge had never been the answer.

It had always been love.

"I'm steady," she said into his hair. "I'm as steady as I have ever been, here in your arms."

She felt the rumble that moved through him, vibrating down to her core. When they reached the tree, their tree, he lightly set her back on the ground.

Letting her go, he brushed a low-hanging branch to the side. "My lady," he said, dipping his chin as a clear invitation for her to enter.

She slid under the canopy, always having loved this spot. While she could see the river, the road was completely blocked from view.

Eric followed behind her, setting down the basket and pulling a blanket from its depths. He unfolded it on the ground before taking her hand again, helping her to sit.

Butterflies danced in her stomach when he sat next to her before leaning back on his elbow. She twisted around to look at him, just liking the sight, but the roguish smile on his face tugged at own lips. "What?"

In answer, he tugged her down, settling her against his body as he kissed her again. The touch lengthened, deepened, as he kissed her over and over, their tongues twining as their bodies pressed together.

This time, however, it was Eric who tugged at his cravat, shedding the fabric. His jacket was next, between kisses, and then his waistcoat.

With every layer, Ella could better feel the definition of his muscles along his torso, her hands exploring them, mapping his body. Until her hands weren't enough. She wanted her body on his body, his skin on hers.

Breaking away from his mouth, she sat up and tugged off her slippers.

"What"—he kissed her shoulder—"are"—then her neck—"you"—the spot behind her ear—"doing?"

She couldn't even lie, couldn't sweeten the truth. "I want to feel your skin."

His mouth stilled. "Ella," he said, his voice coming out a groan, as she gathered up her skirts to untie the ribbons holding her stockings.

Feeling the air on her legs, she lay back, leaving her skirt ruched about her knees. "I know that we ought to wait, but somehow, the road of our courtship has felt long already, and I find myself very impatient."

His answer was to rise on his knees so that he was looking down at her as he tugged his shirt over his head.

And all those rippling muscles were on display.

She drew in a quick breath, her hand rising so that she might trace all the ridges along his stomach, but he hardly gave her a chance as he bent over her, kissing her exposed knee.

She giggled, the ticklish sensation quickly replaced with something far sexier as his lip slid up her leg, his nose pushing her skirts higher.

That ache that had settled between her legs pulsed as his fingers joined the march up her thighs.

He shifted to settle between her legs, his bare shoulders pressing her knees further apart. The feel of his skin against her own made her half sigh, half groan, and she placed one leg over his back, the other against his side, just reveling in the feel of his skin.

His lips slid higher up her thigh, kissing closer and closer to her apex, her body growing more frenzied the further he climbed.

And when his thumb brushed down her seam, she shuddered under the touch, knowing that this was precisely where she was meant to be.

REACHING the apex at the juncture of her legs, Eric flicked his tongue out, giving her a taste. Delicious.

Her body shuddered as her legs tightened about him, and a quick, satisfied grin spread across his lips before he tasted her again.

The touch was a light flick only and he could feel the tension moving through her body as one of her calves hooked around his head, pulling him closer.

He nearly chuckled into her thigh, her eagerness as amusing as it was sexy. This woman belonged with him and he would worship her in the manner befitting her place in his life. His countess...

Flattening his tongue, he licked her again, her body giving a deep shudder as he dragged his tongue up her seam, lingering on the sensitive bud of pleasure.

It would not be difficult to send her over the edge, and while part of him wished to draw this out, they'd have their whole lives for leisure.

Ella had been right—their courtship had been a long, twisted road and they'd waited long enough. Now was the moment to celebrate where they'd finally arrived.

With that in mind, Eric repeated the touch, pushing her legs even further apart so that she shuddered again, her fingers threading into his hair.

That only encouraged him further and soon he was working his tongue over the spot he knew would finish her while he slid a finger into the tight channel of her body.

She clamped down around his digit, giving a keening cry of pleasure. Her finish built, her body trembling with the force of it until she finally broke apart around him.

Satisfaction roared through him as his gaze fixed on her face, the pleasure evident in her panting breaths and taut features. She'd never looked more beautiful.

Rearing up, he came to his knees, looking down at his Ella. Instinctively, he ran a hand over her hip bone, frowning at the way it jutted out. His own pleasure could wait. Ella needed to eat.

But her hooded eyes blinked open, her arms reaching up to him. He found himself coming forward, his hands on either side of her chest as he lowered himself down to kiss her mouth.

And that's when her fingers came to the falls of his breeches.

"No," he murmured against her lips. "When we're married..."

"I told you." She turned her face to the side as she spoke the words. "I don't want to wait any longer, I want to be yours."

His body flared with the same desire, his mind trying to enforce discipline on his body. She was fragile still, both in body and in position. He wanted to take care of her.

But when her hand dipped into his breeches, her palm coming to his cock, his concerns melted away as he tossed his head back, teeth gritted at her touch.

"Love," he ground out. "I want to do the right—"

She cut him off. "Make me yours."

Her words were too much and they shredded the last of his resolve. Kissing her again, he wrapped her hand about his member, guiding her touch. When the energy had built to a point of near breaking, he moved her hand away, pressing the tip into her slick folds.

She stilled under him, her gaze locking with his.

"It's all right, love," he whispered, kissing along her jaw. Frayed as his self control was, he knew that he needed to go slow, make this good for her too.

But her heel pressing into the small of his back made his worries disappear once again as he sank into her.

She was so tight around him, his eyes squeezed shut as he fought to keep his movements slow and controlled.

"Eric," she murmured in his ear. "I'm not a delicate debutante." And then her heel pressed harder.

With one quick movement, he pushed all the way in, fully seating himself in her body. He felt her muscles tighten but she still held him close, her face burrowed in his shoulder. He pulled out, slowly testing her body, and then pushed back in as gently as he could.

Two, three, four more times and then she relaxed around him. The moment he realized that he wasn't causing her pain, the last of his control fell away, and he pushed into her again, his body humming with desire.

Distantly, he was aware that she murmured in his ear but he couldn't hold the words as he moved inside her, his finish building as he held her close.

Squeezing his eyes shut, fingers buried in her golden strands, he breathed in her scent, pushing into her one last time, his climax ripping through him.

Her fingers danced through his hair, her arms and legs twined about him as he collapsed on top of her. He never wanted to move. Ella belonged to him.

She hummed, her languid fingers moving from his hair to his neck and then down his back. Kissing first her cheeks and then her eyes, he slid his mouth over her jaw and into the hollow of her throat.

Which is when he heard her stomach growl.

His head popped up. "You're hungry."

"I'm fine," she whispered back, her eyes sleepy and soft. "Though a nap might be—"

"Food first," he said, pushing up on his hands, and still naked, rolled over to the basket. "You're still recovering and you need to feed your body."

She *tsked* then, but a smile played at her lips. "Sleep is important too."

He pulled a crust of bread and a piece of roast from in the basket and leaned over to kiss her lips before her handing her the food. "Once you've eaten, you can nap against my chest."

She took the food from his hand, and after taking a small bite, lay back on the blanket, smoothing her skirt down her legs. "I suppose I can do that."

"Good." He grabbed another piece of meat, popping it into his mouth. "We've much to do, after all, and you'll need your strength."

"Do?"

"We still have your stepmother to find and capture, and now we've a wedding to plan."

Ella took another bite, the smile slipping from her lips. "Any word on how the search for Vivian is going?"

He shook his head. He shouldn't have brought up the countess. "I'll tell you as soon as I know anything. He pulled on his shirt and sat up against the tree, pulling Ella to his chest. "Now, about our wedding. I'd like it hold it as soon as possible."

"Agreed." She looked up at him, her eyes sparkling. "Fern will be in attendance, obviously. Who else?"

"I have a few friends I'd like to join us."

She gave a quick nod, her food nearly gone, settling more deeply into his chest, her eyes fluttering closed. "Whomever you wish."

He kissed the top of her head, wrapping his arms tighter about her. She was tired, still recovering, and plans could wait. "Sleep now, love. We'll discuss the details when you wake."

"I love you," she softly whispered as her eyes closed.

"I love you too," he returned, his lips grazing her temple.

But her eyes fluttered open again. "Are you tired? Should we return inside? We've been out a long time."

Was she worried that they'd be in danger if they both fell asleep? "Not to worry, love. I'll keep you safe." It was the truth. He understood everything now, and he'd do all that was in his power to protect the woman he loved.

CHAPTER FIFTEEN

Two more days passed in a flurry.

Fern helped Ella to plan the wedding, a simple affair with family, a few friends, and a neighbor or two.

She and Fern sat reviewing the menu for the wedding as Eric came striding into the room. The sight of him still made her catch her breath. He always looked so tall, strong, and handsome, his shoulders filling a doorway as he looked down at them. "I've got news."

"News?" she asked, rising to cross to him.

His brow pulled into a subtle frown. "Have you eaten?"

"For heaven's sake, yes." She did appreciate how he always seemed to care for her needs, though. "Now tell me the news."

"My hired men have traced your stepmother and stepsister to a boat bound for France. They'll follow and apprehend them within the week."

Fern jumped up with a clap and Ella spun to her sister, her brows rising. Fern never expressed such excitement. But then the reason became clear. "Does this mean we don't need to cancel the ball?"

Her eyes widened in surprise. "You want to have a ball?"

"No." Fern wrinkled her nose, making a disgusted face. "I don't want to write all those notes explaining that we've postponed. Better to just get the thing over."

Now, that sounded like Fern. Ella found herself smiling both in relief at Eric's news and excitement. Not only was she getting married, she was going to host a ball.

She'd not even realized she wished for one until it was clear that they'd have it. "We could use the event to announce our engagement," she said with a shy smile at Eric.

He gave her a sidelong glance. "Make a grand announcement? Interesting." His hand shot out to hook her waist. "It was Vivian's plan."

"Just with a different bride," Fern snorted. "The only problem is that we don't have gowns."

But that only made Ella smile wider. "We've got an entire room of them and I don't think Melisandre's coming back to collect them."

Fern's eyes lit with understanding. "Oh, that would be fitting."

"Fitting?" Eric chuckled. "Do you see? The dress both has to fit and taking Melisandre's gown fits the situation."

Fern rolled her eyes and distinctly muttered, "Men are so juvenile."

Which only made both Ella and Eric laugh. "I think a ball is a grand idea," Ella said, laughing all the more at the word *grand*. "Not only can we announce our engagement, but we can introduce Fern for her future coming out."

"No." Fern wagged a finger. "Absolutely not."

But Ella had been taken with the idea. "But you'd said you wished to marry."

"When I thought Vivian would pair me with some toad. Now..." She looked over at Eric. "Unless you insist, my lord. I would not..."

But Eric waved his hand. "I'm insisting on nothing, Fern. But I do think you ought to have a season, if not this year, then next. Why not keep your options open?"

Fern wrinkled her nose again but said nothing. Ella shifted closer to her fiancé. One by one her dreams were coming true.

He pulled her against his chest, his lips grazing her cheek as he ducked to whisper in her ear. "Don't push Fern too hard. She's not the fighter you are and she'll need time to find herself. Trust me."

Ella gave a quick nod. It was her nature to push, but once again, Eric reminded her to love her sister rather than fight with her. "Fern, shall we go look at Melisandre's gown? I can do some alterations for both of us, perhaps piece a few of the dresses together?'

Fern gave a quick nod and then Ella slipped from Eric's arms. "Eric, can you check the breakfast menu for the wedding? I've written the last of the notes, I think. Both of your friends have been invited."

He moved to the desk, his gaze squinting over the list.

Fern stopped, looking back at the table. "I said herring," she murmured, "but Ella was thinking mutton." Fern's fingers slid over the paper. "It pairs nicely with the asparagus, I think."

Eric followed her finger and all at once, Ella realized that Fern knew that Eric struggled and was trying to help him. Gratitude over-whelmed her to know that her sister was attempting to aid without calling Eric out in any way.

Eric gave Fern an easy smile. "Thank you, Fern." Then he gestured toward the door. "Now go pick out some gowns. I can guarantee that reworking them will take longer than it does for me to review the meal."

Fern acknowledged him as Ella reached out her hand to her sister. They left the room in silence, and only when they'd made it around the first corner did she turn to Fern. "How did you know he struggled?"

She shrugged. "His mouth moves when he reads," she quietly responded.

Ella's eyes widened. When had Fern become so observant? "He struggles more with numbers than words." She linked her arm through her sister's. "Thank you for being so tactful. He considers it a failing."

Fern snorted. "Please. He can do what we never could. The man shouldn't feel bad about anything."

Ella couldn't agree more. "Don't tell anyone."

"Who am I going to tell?" Fern replied but then she shook her head. "Even if I could, I wouldn't. Eric is our family now and he has my allegiance, same as you."

She stopped, pulling her sister to her. "Thank you."

Fern hugged her back before they made their way into the dressing room.

The box with the single slipper sat in its place, the one glass shoe winking up at them. "It's a pity you couldn't wear the slippers."

Ella shook her head. "I never wanted to wear them. I only wanted to make Melisandre understand what it meant to go without. Now I think I shall take the single shoe and mount it in a box as a reminder to remain humble."

Fern reached into the box. "That is an excellent idea." She perused the rows of gowns. "Do you think Eric would allow me to sell some of these so that I could provide for my own future?"

Ella squinted at her sister. "Waste not, want not... I understand your sentiment, but all the same." She crossed her arms. "You don't need to provide for yourself."

"I don't blame you for wanting me to marry so that you might have time with Eric without your sister underfoot. I'll find something else to do with myself."

Ella moved to her sister. "I like you underfoot. I only said you should marry because I want you to be happy."

Then she reached for a cornflower-blue silk gown. "Look at this dress... It's perfect for your eyes."

"Or yours," Fern reasoned. "We've the same color eyes."

But Ella was already thumbing through the gowns, her breath catching at a silver concoction, the fabric so light, it floated like a cloud.

Fern gasped. "You must wear that."

"I'll need to take it in..." She held it up to her body, moving closer to the mirror. It brought out the specks in her blue eyes and pinks of her skin. It was meant to be off the shoulder, with small sleeves that wrapped about the underarms. The silk had a sparkly sheen that looked like a jewel in the sunlight. How would it look when the room was lit with candles?

"I've never seen that gown before," Fern said as she came closer, running a hand over the skirts. "When did Melisandre purchase this?"

"I don't know," Ella answered honestly. "Unless..." She nipped at her lip. "Was this to be her wedding dress?"

Fern let out a sharp bark of laughter. "Oh, Ella. You really did manage to steal it all."

Ella looked at the stunning gown. She supposed she had. "It doesn't give me the satisfaction I thought it would. But your and Eric's happiness..." She turned to her sister. "You should wear this. I'll take the blue."

Fern shook her head. "She's got one in here that's a midnight blue that I've always admired." Fern glanced down the row of gowns. "So much waste."

"You're right there. It was one of Melisandre's least attractive traits."

"She did have many." Fern pulled out the dress she wished to wear.

Ella looked at her sister, knowing that Melisandre wasn't the only one who had changes to make. She had a few of her own. "And we'll counter her heartlessness by making decisions with ours. From now on, Fern, we lead with our hearts."

Fern gave a her a small smile that didn't reach her eyes. "I don't even need a life filled with hearts and love. I'll happily settle for a bit of security."

"You have it," Ella answered, knowing that Eric would never force her sister to marry or even leave. "Take some time to think about what will make you happy, Fern."

Fern silently affirmed that as she came up next to Ella, holding the dress in front of her. "We look like night and day with these two gowns," Fern said as she cocked her head to the side, inspecting the dress.

"Put it on. I'll see where I need to trim."

Fern stepped behind the screen. "I'm not saying that I'm looking forward to the ball, but it will be nice not to be shut away during an event."

"I agree," Ella answered, setting the silver gown aside as Fern came back out. Ella gasped to see her sister transformed. Granted, the dress needed to be taken in, but the effect was still obvious. The dark color highlighted Fern's even skin and her sharp blue eyes.

Reaching for some pins, she started to pinch and tuck the dress. "I'll have to turn it inside out at some point, but this will give me an idea."

Fern inspected herself in the mirror. "I like it. I'll be able to hide away in the shadows if I choose."

Ella glanced up at her sister. "Ferns prefer the light."

"Not this Fern," her sister answered. "When are we fitting you?"

"Don't worry. I'll get my turn." Ella was far more interested in her sister's appearance at the moment. With Vivian gone, it was time to move forward into the future.

A soft knock sounded at the door. "It's me," Eric called.

"Come in," she answered, sticking several more pins into the dress.

Only it wasn't Eric who entered, but four maids. Eric called from the other side of the door. "You ladies should try to remember that we have staff at your disposal."

Ella laughed. That was going to take some adjusting...

CHAPTER SIXTEEN

Eric lay in his room listening intently for the sound of Ella returning to the adjoining chamber. With Vivian gone, Fern had moved to a new, far more appropriate room, but Ella had remained next door. They'd set the date for their wedding for ten days from now, and he was struggling to maintain any distance from her.

Now that they'd been intimate, secured their future together, he couldn't seem to keep his hands off of her.

He grinned just thinking about the nights they'd shared. Ella grew more confident with each one, her strength of character and bold nature making her an excellent bedmate and tying his heart more fully to hers.

The door to her room softly opened and then closed once again. He was off his own bed in a second, striding toward the connecting door as he grabbed a passing candle.

He entered her room to find her sitting at the vanity, unpinning her hair.

Without a word, he stood behind her, setting down the candle. Her hands dropped, already knowing that he'd take the pesky little pins out for her. He loved the feel of her silky tresses against his rougher skin, loved to watch the hair fall about her shoulders.

But before he started, he leaned down, kissing the velvet skin of her neck. "How was the fitting?"

She gave him a glowing smile. "I can't wait for you to see the dress."

"I've seen the dress," he rumbled in answer, nipping at the spot between her neck and shoulder. "I am, however, excited to see it on you."

That made her laugh, a breathy sound that moved through him, tightening his muscles as he straightened to begin working her hair free.

She tipped back, her eyes closing while his fingers massaged her scalp. "We're the same height, so no hemming required, but it had to be taken in at the waist and shoulders but let out in the..." Her voice drifted off.

But he only chuckled. "In the chest?" He was well aware that despite her thin frame, her breasts were...ample.

Perhaps he'd need to explore them this evening just to test his theory.

"Yes," she said, a breathy laugh bubbling from her lips when she looked away. Did she feel shy about her endowments? She needn't, he worshipped every inch of her.

Pulling the last of the pins from her hair, he threaded his fingers into her tresses, his fingertips sliding over her scalp and then down her neck, over her back, around her waist.

Her head tilted back to rest on his stomach, giving him an ample view of the breasts he'd just been discussing.

Sliding his hands up her ribcage, he took them both in his hands, Ella reaching up behind herself to hold his waist while he cupped her breasts, his thumbs brushing across both her nipples.

Her gasp, coupled with the arch of her back, had the blood rushing in his veins as he bent low again to kiss the top her head.

She arched her chin up even further until her lips found his. The kiss, all odd angles, was messy, but full of their passion. Eric only broke it because he wanted more of her, her body against his, her skin sliding along his own.

He tore at her buttons, her stockings and ribbons, until she stood before him in nothing but a chemise.

A growl of satisfaction ripped from his mouth as he yanked at his own clothes. She didn't look shy now, in fact, *wanton* was the only word to describe the way her greedy eyes took in his skin.

And the moment he'd stripped to nothing but his breeches, she launched herself into his arms. He caught her easily against his chest. Pulling the length of her along his much larger frame, her feel dangled down against his shins until she wrapped them about his waist.

He walked toward the bed, his hands full of her ass as he massaged the flesh, their tongues tangled together as well.

He paused for a moment, tempted to fall into the bed as he'd done the last several nights, his weight on hers, his hips settling heavily into the cradle of her thighs.

But tonight he wished for something different, and knowing she'd enjoy it, he turned around, his back falling onto the bed with her weight settling on top of him.

She gasped as the thick length of his rod pressed into her soft parts, her body automatically rocking to chase the pleasure.

He gritted his teeth, satisfaction and desire pushing his hips up to make it even better for her.

Her neck and back arched as she repeated the movement. And much as he knew she could finish just like this, it would be so much better for both of them if he were seated inside her.

Pushing her up, which only made her settle onto his cock even more fully, he yanked the chemise over her head, revealing her slender body and large breasts. He reached out, cupping them both before he sat up to take first one nipple and then the second into his mouth, sucking them into stiff peaks as she continued to rock against him.

Finally, when she could take no more, she started tugging at the buttons on the falls of his breeches. He let out a satisfied rumble as he jerked the garment down his hips. They only made it as far as his knees before she was pulling at him to roll over and claim the top.

But he held firm, giving her a smile that was full of male satisfaction as he grasped her hip to lift her up and then used his other hand to guide himself into her entrance.

She sank down on him and when he'd gone all the way to the hilt, her sensitive bud meeting his pubic bone, she let out a low moan that was so sensual, he grasped both her hips, pulling her down even tighter.

Her hands came to his chest, her fingers digging into flesh as she finally pulled up and sank back down.

Her eyes rolled back as her body arched into him. "Eric," she moaned in a way that had him panting to control his own desire.

"That's it, love." He held her hips tight in his hands. "Take your pleasure."

She did, riding him hard and fast, until she came with a desperate, keening cry that had hardly receded before he flipped her over, pumping into her with such abandon that his own release stole the air from his lungs.

He collapsed on top of her and then rolled to the side, dragging her against his side, coiling an arm around her back to keep her warm and safe.

She curled like a kitten into him, purring his name before she fell fast asleep.

It only took a minute to join her. But his last thought was that he was exactly where he belonged and that he'd give this woman every piece of himself before he'd allow anything to harm her ever again.

CHAPTER SEVENTEEN

ELLA SAT AT THE VANITY, eyes closed, her hair being tugged and pulled with such force that tears stung her eyes. Eric was so much gentler when he worked the strands out of the pins.

As Mary, her new maid, put them in, they scraped and poked. "Mary," she said through gritted teeth, not wanting to hurt the girl's feelings but also tired of being poked like a pin cushion, "I'm sure what you've done is fine—"

"Just a few more," Mary answered, sounding a bit strained. "I've almost got it."

Ella pressed her lips together but remained silent as Mary finally stepped back. "There."

Ella opened her eyes and nearly gasped in shock. Her hair was magnificent. Loosely pulled back, each curl twisted and pinned to look effortlessly tousled and yet artfully arranged, the style softening her features in the most feminine way. "Oh, Mary."

"I know, Lady Ella, you'll be the belle of this ball, I'm certain."

Ella's belly fluttered with nerves. She hoped so. She'd spent so long cast in the shadows of society that she wondered how she was going to feel to be part of that world once again.

She'd wanted this, but now that she had it—would she feel like she actually belonged here?

Somehow, Mary's work eased some of the tension. She'd look the part, anyhow. Mary helped her into the silver dress, the gown now displaying a good amount of décolletage before it cinched in at the waist, displaying her feminine curves. Her eyes danced in the candle-light, and Mary pinched Ella's cheeks, adding some color to them, then lifted the skirts to help Ella slide her feet into the waiting slippers.

"How do I look?"

"Like a princess," Mary gushed, clasping her hands in front of her heart.

Ella laughed. "I don't need to look like a princess. But hopefully, I'll pass for a future countess." She twisted in the mirror, watching how the gown caught the light and sparkled. Its lines were simple enough, not Melisandre's usual taste but the fabric was breathtaking.

Mary helped her into her crisp white elbow gloves, and then Ella started down the hall to find Fern.

Her sister looked stunning as well, the midnight-blue gown only highlighting her fair hair and blue eyes, and Ella gave a small clap to see her.

Fern only wrinkled her nose. "Don't get any ideas."

"Ideas?" she asked, threading her arm through her sister's.

"I know you're in love and happy, but that doesn't mean all of us want that future."

Ella pressed her lips together. She did happen to think that her sister should open herself to love, but that wasn't the real source of her happiness. "I just like seeing you like this. We've found ourselves on the other side of Vivian's cruelty. It's been so long coming that I thought we might never make it."

Fern made a soft noise of agreement. "You're right there." Then she stopped and leaned in to kiss her sister's cheek. "Thank you."

"You're welcome," Ella answered as they reached the top of the stairs. Guests already milled about the entry and Eric waited at the bottom, greeting people as they entered. He stood with another man, as tall and broad as himself. Ella knew him, having met him a few times, the Marquess of Millbury. He lived within a half day's ride from here, and Vivian had considered him a potential suitor for Melisandre until he'd refused in what Ella had heard was a very direct manner.

But the marquess was forgotten as her gaze moved to Eric once again. Her breath caught to see him in his black formal wear, his jacket barely containing his shoulders.

His eyes drifted up to her and he stopped, staring.

She pressed a hand down her skirt, her chin dipping as she fought back a wave of insecurity. Would he think that she looked like the countess he needed her to be?

She lifted her eyes again to meet his gaze, his dark eyes unreadable but his body giving off an intensity that stole her breath as he lifted a hand up, inviting her to his side.

Fern let go of her arm, giving Ella's elbow the slightest squeeze. "Go."

She did, floating down the stairs toward him, and when her gloved fingers slipped into his, she let out a breath.

"Lady Ella," Eric murmured. "May I introduce you to the Marquess of Millbury."

She dipped into a curtsy. "It's good to see you again, my lord."

"Have me met?" The marquess eyed her up and down, his deep baritone echoing through the entry. He was a large man, his features harshly handsome, craggy and a tad menacing. "Surely, I would remember such an enchanting creature."

Eric's hand tightened on hers as he took a half step between her and the marquess. She nearly laughed at the absurdity of his jealousy. No man could even compare to him. "You've met?" Eric asked, glaring at the marquess but clearly addressing his question to her.

"A few times. You were acquainted with my stepmother and stepsister, Lady Melisandre."

His eyes widened in surprise and his gaze flicked to Fern, who'd come to stand next to her. "Right," he murmured, bowing his head to Fern. "How nice to see you both again. I was sorry to hear of your father and my apologies for not attending the funeral. I was away on business."

Ella did not ask what business a marquess might be in, nor did she care that he hadn't attended. The marquess moved on as Eric glared at his back. "He met you and he did nothing to help?"

Fern shrugged. "The meetings were always very brief and then Vivian sent us off. Like she tried to do with you."

"Still," Eric started, his gaze hardening, "he should have..."

"Not all men are as honorable and heroic as you."

"Don't make me sick." Fern made a gagging sound, though her lips pulled into a small smile.

He quirked a brow at Fern before he placed a hand at the small of her back. "I think we ought to make our announcement just before dinner." His fingers pressed into her waist. "Tell me I can have your dinner dance."

"You can have all my dances," she answered, knowing she likely had a foolish grin on her face. It was just that she'd met the most perfect man, and here she stood proudly at his side in a beautiful gown, transformed. She would never wish to be anywhere else with anyone else.

Eric was her present and her future.

———

THE EVENING PASSED with a smooth grace, Eric relaxing with every hour that ticked by. He'd gone for simple dishes, hoping to keep down the cost of the event.

Granted, the found money from his viscountcy had gone a long way in easing his financial burden and with any luck, the money Vivian had stolen would be found as well. But he and Ella seemed to have an unspoken agreement that the path forward was one of frugal caution and careful spending.

But if tonight's guests minded, they didn't allow it to show. Instead, they welcomed the new earl and fawned over Fern and Ella, no one outright speaking ill of Vivian but many expressing their satisfaction at seeing the sisters back in the ballroom.

As the time for his dance with Ella approached, he found himself scanning the ballroom, looking for her.

It wasn't difficult to spot her. She was the gem of the evening, and everywhere she went a crowd of men and women seemed to follow her. He knew the jealousy that had beat in his chest was irrational, but he supposed his old insecurities still lingered. Would she prefer a smarter man? One who could give her a future that did not involve the compromises he required?

Tugging as his jacket, he found her just before their dance, a ring of men smiling at her as he swept between them, holding out his hand to her.

He could hardly wait to announce their engagement, wanting to claim her for his own.

She gave him a warm smile, her hand slipping into his, her cheek brushing his shoulder as he led her away from her ring of admirers.

"I know that it will be a late night, but I need you in my bed tonight." His hand came to her back as he subtly trailed his fingers down her spine.

"There isn't anywhere I'd rather be."

It was the catch in her voice, the way her eyes shone at him, that uncoiled the tension in his chest. Despite the fact that he felt inadequate when faced with all this competition, she looked at him as though he'd hung the moon.

Holding her in his arms, the music began and the rest of the ballroom melted away as he spun her about the floor.

Her small frame looked so fragile in his hands and arms that he pulled her a touch tighter, wanting to protect her. On and on they spun, and while Eric desperately wanted to announce their engagement, another part of him wished to sweep her outside onto the veranda, where he could pull her into the shadows and kiss her senseless.

But he stayed in the ballroom, consoling himself that they could sneak out for just a few moments after the announcement but before dinner.

And with that, he pulled Ella toward the small orchestra, grabbing two glasses of champagne as the staff began to pass them about.

Clinking on his glass, others followed until the room fell silent.

"Thank you to all of you who have come to welcome me into the earldom. It has been an honor meeting everyone. I look forward to getting to know all of you better in my coming days as earl and my doors are open to you for whatever you need." Many on the list were local neighbors and surrounding peerage. A murmur of acceptance moved through the crowd as he reached for Ella's hand, pulling her closer. "I'd also like to announce that Lady Ella Cartwright has consented to be my wife."

A much louder roar moved through the crowd, with a fair number of calls punctuating it.

Everyone raised their glasses and then Eric brought his to his lips, watching as Ella did the same, her gaze locked with his.

His chest swelled with pride to know that this woman was his, that they'd be wed by this time next week and that his life had finally fallen into order.

With that in mind, as the guests finished their champagne and started for the dining room, he took her hand and pulled her outside.

CHAPTER EIGHTEEN

THE COOL NIGHT air felt marvelous against Ella's skin as Eric pulled her outside. A few other couples milled about the large veranda but Eric passed them all, moving to the south end of the house where the ballroom cast little light into the darkness.

"Eric," she giggled, trying to keep up with his long strides. "We'll be missed."

"It's only for a few minutes and then we'll go back inside. I need to kiss you."

Those words trilled along her spine, sending sparks and need coursing through her. She needed to kiss him too. His announcement, the public proclamation that he'd chosen her...it had filled her heart with so much love. For so long, she'd been fed by hate. Choosing this path, him, the feelings that flowed between them, needed to be celebrated, and kissing seemed like the perfect way to do it.

He pulled her against his chest, his lips finding hers as she twined her arms about his neck.

His tongue plundered her mouth, her fingers twined into his hair.

Leaving her mouth, he began kissing a trail down her cheek, to her jaw, and then her neck, his tongue tasting at her skin as she gasped in a breath. "Tonight was so perfect," she whispered into the night. "I never dreamed…"

"Didn't you, though?" Her stepmother's voice made her gasp and she stiffened in Eric's arms.

"Vivian," she said, pushing away and spinning around. Her stepmother was close, and as Ella searched the darkness, she found the other woman's outline where she leaned against the house. "What are you doing here?"

"Thought I was on some boat?" Vivian pushed off the wall. "I still have allies and friends, you know—even in this house."

"They'll find the money, wherever you've hidden it," Eric growled out.

"Pity you couldn't just marry Melisandre."

"And be your puppet, just like your husband?" Eric spoke through gritted teeth. "You seem like a smart woman, but your plan was so flawed…"

Vivian snorted. "I didn't have much choice. With Ella reaching the age of twenty, her father had begun to develop a spine. Couldn't have that."

"But…" Ella's stomach twisted into knots. "But now you've ruined everything."

"You ruined everything." Vivian's voice rose louder and grew higher-pitched.

Ella moved closer to Eric, grasping his arm. "I didn't kill an earl or attempt to steal his money."

Vivian lifted her hand to expose a small pistol fitted into her palm. "You would have if you could. We all know what a little thief you are."

"I stole what I needed to survive, not out of greed," Ella bit back.

"You don't fool me, girl. You and I are creatures cut from the same cloth."

Ella winced at those words, her heart sinking into her toes. They touched that deep place in her heart that worried Vivian's accusation was true.

But it was Eric who answered. "You wish that was true because if it was, your treatment of your stepdaughter might be justified. But we both know that it took years of manipulation and neglect that pushed her so far into a corner—"

"Shut up." Vivian raised the gun higher, jabbing it in Eric's direction.

"You can silence me, but that doesn't change the fact that you are done. It's only a matter of time before you're caught. You'll go to prison and Melisandre will have to marry any man that will take her."

"You leave my daughter out of this." Vivian's voice was so high, it was practically a shriek. "If you had any idea what my first husband was like, you'd know that Ella and I are the same..." Vivian tapered off with a shake of her head. "One of you is going to die tonight. If I'm finished, I'm taking someone with me." She pointed the pistol first at Eric and then at Ella. "I couldn't decide at first, but then..." The grin that curled her lips was pure evil.

Ella shivered, her hand tightening on his arm. She was afraid for herself but as he straightened up, his lip curling in anger, fear for Eric made Ella rigid with worry. "Vivian, I'm sure we can come to some sort of arrangement. You return the money and we'll—"

"You'll decide which one of you dies." Vivian hurled the words at her with a cackle of laughter. "Will you have me kill him, Ella? Do you think you can seduce the next heir and still become a countess?"

Seduction? That had been Ella's plan. She couldn't deny it. But now...standing next to him, it was overwhelming love that made her let go of his arm, step in front of him, and spread her arms wide. "I don't care about being a countess, Vivian," she answered softly. "But I won't let you hurt him."

Vivian's face contorted for a moment, looking truly hideous before a calm, cold mask fell over her features. "As you wish."

And then her finger slipped over the trigger.

A scream filled her throat a second before she fell to the side, her body hitting the stone at the same moment that the gun let out an ear-splitting crack.

Eric stood tall for a moment and then he was crumpling forward. A scream built in her throat as Vivian went flying in the opposite direction as them, a large shadow tackling her to the ground.

Ella scrambled to her knees, heedless of the pain in her shoulder when she scrambled to Eric's side. He was already sitting up, his face twisted in pain as he looked down at his arm.

"What's wrong?" she gasped. He ripped off his coat and tore at his sleeve.

With a grimace, he looked down at his arm. "She managed to graze—"

"She shot you?" Ella cried, her trembling fingers moving to his arm as she squinted down at the wound. "Eric!"

"Ella, it's fine," he hushed her. "It's only a graze." And then he wrapped his other arm about her, pulling her close. "How could you put yourself in front of me like that?"

"I.." She swallowed down a lump. "I love you. How could you..." Pain lanced her chest. "How could you take that bullet meant for me. I..." She couldn't say more, her chest was so tight.

"I would never let anyone hurt you, ever."

Had she ever questioned whether this man was strong enough to keep her safe? She wrapped her arms about his neck, burying her face into his shoulder. "Oh, Eric."

"Sorry to interrupt," a dry male voice called from the shadows. "But she'll wake soon and we ought to have her subdued before that."

Ella blinked into the darkness. The marquess stood just in the shadows, Vivian's crumpled form at his feet. "My lord," she gasped, pushing to her feet. "Was it you who helped us?"

He shrugged. "Right place, right time."

Eric pushed up too, pulling his shirt over his head. "What are you doing?" she asked, looking at his arm in alarm.

He handed her the shirt. "It's ruined anyway. Tear it into pieces so that we can use it to bind her and then we'll fetch the authorities." He looked down at his arm. "And leave a few pieces for me. I might need them..."

Ela began to rip, taking a few large pieces, and then tossed the shirt to the marquess. "Would you mind, my lord? I'd like to wrap my fiancé's arm."

"Of course, my lady," he answered, catching the shirt easily and ripping several more sections.

Ella gently but firmly wrapped the bleeding wound. "I'm worried about you."

"Don't be," he said as he touched her forehead. "I'll be fine. Better than that, Vivian has been caught and we can truly put this all behind us before we're wed."

A lightness she'd not felt in years settled over her at those words. Vivian would be in prison and she'd found the love of her life. Truly, she was blessed.

Wrapping her arms about his waist, she pulled them together. "I love you."

He brought a hand to her hair, kissing her temple. "I love you too."

Her eyes squeezed shut and then slowly opened again, another cry falling from her lips.

"What's wrong?" Eric asked, pushing her back in concern, his gaze searching up and down her body.

"The dress," she cried, pointing to a rip. "It's ruined."

"Ruined?"

"I wanted to marry you in this dress," she whispered as she poked at the hole. Then she stepped into his arms again.

"Ella," he murmured into her hair. "The dress doesn't matter."

She nodded. "I know. I'd marry you in my chemise, but still... I wanted to be the woman you deserved."

"You are," he answered, holding her tighter. "And so much more, my love."

That made her smile. It was over and this man belonged to her.

EPILOGUE

ONE WEEK LATER...

ERIC STOOD at the front of the church waiting for his bride. Outwardly, he appeared patient, but inside...a riot of emotions made it near impossible to stay still.

"You haven't blinked in over a minute," Nick, more formally known as the Duke of Wingate, said as he slapped Eric on the back. "Nervous?"

"No," he answered honestly. Nervous was not the correct word. He was anxious to see this done, thrilled to make Ella his bride, excited for the future—all of which made him shake his head. What had happened to the lovable rake who had rode to Castleton?

But he knew that man had been a lie. This man, who stood at the front of the church, was his true self. Flawed but trying his best to be a good man, a hardworking and loving partner to a beautiful woman.

"You've barely said a word all morning. What's wrong, if you're not nervous?" Jacob asked. The baron stood on the other side of Nick, his gaze straying to where Fern stood in the back of the church with Nick's wife, Aubrey, and Aubrey's best friend, Emily.

126

Briefly, he wondered which woman Jacob was eyeing. Whispers broke out among the women and then Emily came rushing to the front of the church, a wide smile on her face. Eric had only met the delicately beautiful brunette a few days ago, but she was an easy woman to like. Warm, kind, gentle. She didn't have the sort of strength that a woman like Ella or even Fern had. And Nick's wife, Aubrey, was a survivor for certain, but still... He liked Emily a great deal.

And the way Jacob's eyes followed her up the aisle, seeming to drink her in, told Eric that his friend might feel far more than just a liking for this woman.

"She's here," Emily gushed on an excited rush of air. "She's arrived."

Eric let out a long breath he hadn't even realized he was holding. Being near Ella always calmed him and it did so now.

Nick quirked a brow, but Jacob had forgotten all about his friend. "How is your brother, Miss Cranston?"

"Brother?" Eric asked, finding himself more able to make conversation with his bride just outside.

"Baron Aberforth," Jacob said with a shake of his head. "We were good friends at Oxford and you would have liked him too, if you'd attended."

Eric didn't answer. He'd not told his friends about his struggles with the written word, mostly because there hadn't been opportunity but also because Fern and Ella knowing seemed like enough. At least for now.

"My brother is well, as far as I know," Emily answered. "He's been on tour for nearly a year now," she said as she looked up at the ceiling, a smile playing at her lips. "My mother thinks that he's avoiding my father, but my father swears it's my mother he doesn't wish to see."

Jacob eyed Emily up and down, stepping closer. "He's left you alone?"

"Not alone." Emily shook her head. "My parents are with me and if you met my mother, you'd understand just how little time I actually have to myself."

That made her laugh and Jacob smiled too. "I see."

127

"But when next I see my errant brother, I'll send him your regards, Lord Robinson."

"Do," Jacob answered as Emily turned back down the aisle, the women going to meet Ella.

Jacob's gaze followed her the entire way.

Nick made a *tsk*ing noise. "Don't tell me that marriage is contagious?"

Jacob snorted. "If you're referring to me, the answer is definitely not. Just because you two are suckers doesn't mean I need to be."

Nick laughed at that, but Eric gave Jacob a long stare. "If you don't want to wind up wed, you ought to put your eyes back in your head. Emily is not the sort of girl that you can have a meaningless tryst with."

"Says who?" Jacob asked, but it was Nick's hand that knocked into Jacob's shoulder.

"Says me," he answered. "And Eric. Go anywhere near Emily and the two of us will see you wed within the fortnight."

Jacob mumbled something but didn't say more as a hush fell over the church, the guests standing.

And then Ella appeared in the door. He forgot everything else as he stared at her, her pale pink gown making her look as fresh as sunrise and twice as beautiful.

He shifted then. This woman belonged by his side and in just a moment, she'd be exactly there.

And Eric intended to keep her beside him forever.

THE "ALL THAT GLITTERS" series is far from done! In fact, we're just heating up! Up next, The Baron to Break!

THE BARON TO BREAK

There are times in life where change is so slow, it seems as though it isn't happening at all. Miss Emily Cranston, daughter of Viscount and Viscountess Marsden, had spent years hoping to be out from beneath her mother's watchful eye.

And for years, absolutely nothing had changed in this regard. Emily's mother decided which parties she attended, to whom she spoke, what she ate, and when she slept. Emily had secretly begged for the iron hand of her mother to be lifted so that she might choose something, anything for herself.

But now, at the age of twenty, without warning—not even the smallest hint—the greatest change of them all had occurred. Death.

Didn't people often have a premonition in this regard? Some clue, a shiver or a dream or *something* that warned them irrevocable circumstances were about to occur?

She'd received not even the smallest hint…

And in one swift accident, a muddy road and an overturned carriage, she'd lost both her parents, and now Emily found herself alone. A tear slid down her cheek, covered by the veil she still wore on her head.

The funeral had been hours ago, but she'd not bothered to take off the veil, nor had she removed the black gloves that still covered her hands.

Her brother had been gone for months on some tour of Europe, and while word had been sent to him, Emily had no idea when he might return or how long she'd have to drift along these halls without a bit of company. She felt like a ghost in this moment, alone and not really living at all.

No one had prepared her for such an event. She'd been smothered in attention for years. What would she even do alone?

Her mother had been attempting to match Emily with some suitable lord for the last year and a half. Emily had tried her utmost to avoid the matches, not having found any of the men of particular interest.

They'd been older or dull or not particularly handsome. Her mother had regularly thrown up her hands. "Lord Tinderwell owns more land than any duke in England. What's the matter with you?"

"The matter?" she'd ask. Lord Tinderwell was twice her age and not a particularly good conversationalist. Was it wrong for a girl to wish for a bit of adventure? Excitement? Romance, even?

She winced as she blotted more tears from her eyes. If she'd listened to her mother, she wouldn't be in this predicament now.

She'd have her husband's arm about her, facing her parents' deaths, yes. But not the soul-crushing loneliness that filled her.

She lay down on the settee, tucking her hands under her head. She'd written to her best friend, now the Duchess of Wingate. Surely, Aubrey would be able to help her. Keep her company while she waited for her mourning period to end and her brother to return.

And after that? Would her brother help her find a match? He'd never been much for society, despite being the heir.

Perhaps Tinderwell was still available. She sat up. His Grace could write to the man on her behalf, ask for a meeting…

Distantly, she knew these were the acts of a woman who was desperately afraid, but suddenly, she needed some anchor to hold her in place. She was adrift, alone, and adventure sounded like the silly notion of a silly girl who didn't understand just how delightfully secure she'd been.

"Miss Cranston," the butler said softly from the doorway. "I'm sorry to interrupt, but you have visitors."

"Visitors?"

"Your father's solicitor." The butler cleared his throat. "And a second man who claims to be a friend of your brother's, Lord Robinson."

She stood, blinking several times.

The solicitor, she'd expected, though to be fair, she thought he'd not come calling until her brother had arrived.

But Lord Robinson...

She'd met him at a wedding six months prior. It felt like a lifetime ago. Her father had allowed her to attend without her mother, trusting Aubrey and the Duke of Wingate to be her chaperones.

It had been a tantalizing taste of freedom that had elated Emily, though in this moment, her excitement seemed foolish. She ought to have stayed home. Found a suitor— "Send them in."

"Both of them?" the butler asked, his brow furrowing in an unusual display of feeling.

She lifted the hand still holding her kerchief. "Lord Robison is a longtime friend of Ashton's. They attended Oxford together, both speaking fondly of the other." Emily had had very little to do with financial affairs, her parents sheltering her from such dealings. "I'm certain he'll be a great help during this meeting."

The butler gave a stiff nod of assent before he disappeared again, returning with both men. As today had been the funeral, Emily felt it suitable to accept callers offering condolences.

But tomorrow, she'd begin her period of isolation as she mourned. She gave a shiver to think on it.

Lord Robinson entered, Mr. Barrow just behind him. Even through her thick crepe veil, Emily couldn't help but notice how large Lord Robinson was. He had to be more than six feet and his shoulders were so broad.

The urge to hide behind him welled up inside her, though she forced her feet to remain in her spot next to the mantel.

"Miss Cranston," Lord Robinson said, giving a short bow as he took her hand in his. "Allow me to offer my sincere regret for your loss."

She gave a nod, her throat clogging with tears. "Thank you," she managed to whisper.

Mr. Barrow also bowed, offering similar words before his eyes strayed about the room. "No word from the new viscount?"

"No," Emily said with a shake of her head.

"Is there some relative that can join you here?" Lord Robinson asked, his brow furrowing in concern.

Mr. Barrow cleared his throat. "I've written to your great aunt and await a response."

Emily winced to think of the aging woman traveling. Her father's sister and widow to the Marquess of Delvin, she was too old to make such a journey. "Thank you. I've written to the Duke and Duchess of Wingate. Perhaps when they arrive, they can escort me to her estate."

"Excellent," he said as Emily gestured for everyone to sit. Lord Robinson sat next to her on the settee while Mr. Barrow took the seat across from them. A tea service was brought in and she began to pour the cups automatically, as her mother had taught her to do.

"There are matters which we need to discuss," Mr. Barrow added between sips of tea. "But I'd rather hoped to have your brother here before we began."

"Then we shall be drinking a lot of tea, I think," she answered with a shake of her head.

Lord Robinson gave a small laugh, his gaze darting to her and then back to Mr. Barrow. "Is Miss Cranston provided for financially while she awaits her brother's return?"

"Yes," Mr. Barrow answered. "If he doesn't return—"

"Doesn't return!" Emily cried, the thought of her brother not coming back more than she could bear. Her vision grew grey around the edges and she felt herself sway until a steadying hand came to her back, another grasping her fingers in a large palm.

She knew it was Lord Robinson's large hand that engulfed hers even as she had the urge to sink into the strength of his embrace. "He'll return," came his quiet baritone. He sounded so confident, so self-assured that she drew in a deep breath. She'd needed him to say that.

"Thank you," she answered, trying to draw in another deep breath, draw up the strength this conversation, this day required.

Lord Robinson's hand was still on her back. "Why don't you let me speak with Mister Barrow. I'll check in on you before I leave."

Oh, that sounded wonderful. She wanted to rise to the occasion, but she felt as though she were sinking. With a quick nod of ascension, Lord Robinson helped her up and out the door. "I'll just be in the study across the hall," she murmured as he stayed by her side, strong hand at her back, helping her into the room and then into a chair.

"Close your eyes and rest. I'll be in soon."

She gave a quick nod and did exactly as he'd requested.

———

Jacob cursed himself a thousand times as he looked down at that damn veil covering her face. Emily was a fragile and protected beauty and on the few occasions they'd met, he could not deny that he felt her appeal. Intimately.

But until this morning, he'd kept the feeling well within check. He was not the sort of man who dallied with a viscount's daughter. Not an eligible one, anyway.

He liked his life just as it was, which was free of entanglement, devoid of commitment, and full of pleasure.

But when he'd heard about Emily's loss...

Not even he was cold-hearted enough to leave her to face this day alone. Damn Ashton. Where the hell was her brother? He ought to have come back by now, loss or no.

Jacob returned to the sitting room, Mr. Barrow looking decidedly irritable as he fidgeted with his glasses and adjusted his pocket watch.

"My lord," the man began before Jacob had even sat, "there was little point in seeing the lady off."

"Why is that?"

"The details are not for you to discuss." The man somehow looked down his nose at Jacob despite being several inches shorter.

"Which details are those?" he asked, wishing for something stronger than tea. He knew it was a bad habit to drink as often as he did, but then again, life so often disappointed. He scraped a hand through his overlong hair.

"The ones that pertain to my client. I ought not to share them with anyone other than the new viscount." The man continued to fidget, pulling at his waistcoat and straightening his cravat. "The problem is that Miss Cranston has—" He stopped, his lips pressing together.

Jacob sighed. He understood the solicitor's dilemma. Still, Jacob could not help Emily if he didn't know of any potential problems. And for some ludicrous reason, he was intent upon helping her.

It was his loyalty to Ashton. The man had pulled him from more scrapes than Jacob cared to count. Jacob had been troubled as a child, shunted off from school to school because they'd not keep him and his mother didn't wish for him to be home.

At times, Ashton had felt like his only family, though he had a father and a brother besides. Not that any of them acted like a family.

But Ashton had supported him with friendship when few others had and this was Jacob's chance to repay his friend.

Besides, Emily seemed so fragile, and what was happening to her might lay even the strongest low. He'd not allow himself to get so tangled that he'd forget who and what he was: a man who did not allow himself to become attached to anyone.

Ever.

And he wouldn't to Emily. He was a seasoned rake and she was just an innocent debutante. Hardly seasoned at all.

A small voice argued the point. He found her innocence refreshing, captivating even. But he turned off that voice. This was Ashton's sister, and besides, innocence quickly faded and then he'd be left with the same sort of woman he knew well.

He wasn't meant to be tied to any female's apron strings.

Assured that he was not in danger of compromising his way of life, he gave Barrow an easy smile. "Mister Barrow, between you and me, I was in the process of negotiating with the viscount when his untimely death interrupted."

"Negotiating?"

Jacob gave a grimace that he quickly covered. He needed to know what was happening, which meant misleading Mr. Barrow into giving him information. Jacob would like to say that this was a first, but he was rather adept at fooling people into acting as he wished.

Which meant he knew the pitfalls to avoid.

"Emily and I..." He lifted his brows. He'd not say *engaged*. He was speaking to a solicitor and he'd have preferred if the man inferred meaning rather than Jacob outwardly saying words he'd have to retract later. But he wanted Barrow to think it. He wanted the man to know that in Ashton's absence, Jacob was the man to trust.

Mr. Barrow's eyes widened, his hands smoothing down his middle. "I see."

Jacob could practically see him calculating behind his spectacles, his pupils quickly moving left to right. And then he seemed to relax. "All around, that makes everything easier."

Jacob had to agree.

Of course, he wasn't engaged to Emily, nor would he ever be, but Ashton would surely forgive the fib when he learned that Jacob only wished to protect the man's sister. "So tell me. What should I know?"

"Well, if you were negotiating a dowry, then you're aware already."

Jacob lifted his brows. Know what? But he didn't say a word. He found that silence often forced the other person to begin speaking.

Which is exactly what Mr. Barrow did. "But perhaps you'd not reached that point yet in your negotiations."

"Perhaps," he replied, again not committing to anything.

Mr. Barrow cleared his throat. "They hid it well, but Miss Cranston is very short on funds."

Jacob held completely still, as though this information wasn't shocking in the least. So sweet, tempting Emily was without a protector or money? Fuck. "How short?"

Mr. Barrow shrugged. "She'll need to find a relative willing to provide for her until her brother can be found."

"What has been done to locate Ashton?" The man had gone on a tour of Europe a year before. He'd been expected months ago and the fact he wasn't here...

"I'm not privy to those details," Mr. Barrow said and cleared his throat.

Jacob swore under his breath. The situation was worse than he'd imagined. "Rest assured, Mister Barrow, that while our engagement was not public, nor will it be until her mourning period is over, I shall see Emily well protected until her brother returns and can finalize our arrangements."

Mr. Barrow gave a quick jerk of his chin to acknowledge Jacob's words before he rose. "Excellent."

For the briefest moment, Jacob wondered at the distinct frown that marked Mr. Barrow's brow. Was there more he should know? Did Mr. Barrow have reason not to support Jacob's suit? It was fake, of course, but Mr. Barrow didn't know that. And the other man had likely heard of Jacob's reputation.

Hell, not even his own mother liked him, why would Mr. Barrow?

Jacob lifted his hand to show the man out and then started across the hall to see how the lady in question fared and to decide what happened next.

Hell, even he didn't know. This was his first time pretending to be engaged.

Want to read more? The Baron to Break is available on major retailers!

Or starte the All That Glitters series from the beginning with:
The Duke Who Dared!

Keep up with all the latest news, sales, freebies, and releases by joining my newsletter!

www.tammyandresen.com

Hugs!

ABOUT THE AUTHOR

Tammy Andresen lives with her husband and three children just outside of Boston, Massachusetts. She grew up on the Seacoast of Maine, where she spent countless days dreaming up stories in blueberry fields and among the scrub pines that line the coast. Her mother loved to spin a yarn and Tammy filled many hours listening to her mother retell the classics. It was inevitable that at the age of eighteen, she headed off to Simmons College, where she studied English literature and education. She never left Massachusetts but some of her heart still resides in Maine and her family visits often.

Find out more about Tammy:
http://www.tammyandresen.com/
https://www.facebook.com/authortammyandresen
https://twitter.com/TammyAndresen
https://www.pinterest.com/tammy_andresen/
https://plus.google.com/+TammyAndresen/

OTHER TITLES BY TAMMY

Lords of Scandal

Duke of Daring

Marquess of Malice

Earl of Exile

Viscount of Vice

Baron of Bad

Earl of Sin

———————————

Earl of Gold

Earl of Baxter

Duke of Decandence

Marquess of Menace

Duke of Dishonor

Baron of Blasphemy

Viscount of Vanity

Earl of Infamy

Laird of Longing

———————————

Duke of Chance

Marquess of Diamonds

Queen of Hearts

Baron of Clubs

Earl of Spades

King of Thieves

Marquess of Fortune

Calling All Rakes

Wanted: An Earl for Hire

Needed: A Dishonorable Duke

Found: Bare with a Baron

Vacancy: Viscount Required

Lost: The Love of a Lord

Missing: An Elusive Marquess

Wanted: Title of Countess

The Dark Duke's Legacy

Her Wicked White

Her Willful White

His Wallflower White

Her Wanton White

Her Wild White

His White Wager

Her White Wedding

The Rake's Ruin

When only an Indecent Duke Will Do

How to Catch an Elusive Earl

Where to Woo a Bawdy Baron

When a Marauding Marquess is Best

What a Vulgar Viscount Needs

Who Wants a Brawling Baron

When to Dare a Dishonorable Duke

The Wicked Wallflowers

Earl of Dryden

Too Wicked to Woo

Too Wicked to Wed

Too Wicked to Want

How to Reform a Rake
Don't Tell a Duke You Love Him
Meddle in a Marquess's Affairs
Never Trust an Errant Earl
Never Kiss an Earl at Midnight
Make a Viscount Beg

Wicked Lords of London
Earl of Sussex
My Duke's Seduction
My Duke's Deception
My Earl's Entrapment
My Duke's Desire
My Wicked Earl

Brethren of Stone
The Duke's Scottish Lass
Scottish Devil
Wicked Laird
Kilted Sin
Rogue Scot
The Fate of a Highland Rake

A Laird to Love
Christmastide with my Captain
My Enemy, My Earl
Heart of a Highlander
A Scot's Surrender
A Laird's Seduction

Taming the Duke's Heart

Taming a Duke's Reckless Heart

Taming a Duke's Wild Rose

Taming a Laird's Wild Lady

Taming a Rake into a Lord

Taming a Savage Gentleman

Taming a Rogue Earl

Fairfield Fairy Tales

Stealing a Lady's Heart

Hunting for a Lady's Heart

Entrapping a Lord's Love: Coming in February of 2018

American Historical Romance

Lily in Bloom

Midnight Magic

The Golden Rules of Love

Boxsets!!

Taming the Duke's Heart Books 1-3

American Brides

A Laird to Love

Wicked Lords of London

Manufactured by Amazon.ca
Bolton, ON